poachers

tom franklin

POACHERS

stories

William Morrow and Company, Inc.
New York

Some of these stories have appeared, often in a slightly different form or under a different title, in the following publications: *Quarterly West, The Nebraska Review, Fourteen Hills, Brightleaf, Gulf Coast Collection of Stories and Poems, Smoke, The Chattahoochee Review, Negative Capability, Louisiana Literature,* and *The Texas Review.*

It is the policy of William Morrow and Company, Inc., and its imprints and affiliates, recognizing the importance of preserving what has been written, to print the books we publish on acid-free paper, and we exert our best efforts to that end.

Library of Congress Cataloging-in-Publication Data

Franklin, Tom.
    Poachers : stories / Tom Franklin.—1st ed.
      p.   cm.
    Contents: Hunting years—Grit—Shubuta—Triathlon—Blue horses—The ballad of Duane Juarez—A tiny history—Dinosaurs—Instinct—Alaska—Poachers.
    ISBN 0-688-16740-3 (alk. paper)
    1. Southern States—Social life and customs—Fiction.   I. Title.
PS3556.R343P63   1999
813'.54—dc21   98-51982
                                               CIP

Printed in the United States of America

First Edition

   2 3 4 5 6 7 8 9 10

BOOK DESIGN BY BONNI LEON-BERMAN

www.williammorrow.com

For Beth Ann

and for my parents,
Gerald and Betty Franklin

contents

poachers

introduction
hunting years

Standing on a trestle in south Alabama, I look down into the coffee-brown water of the Blowout, a fishing hole I loved as a boy. It's late December, cold. A stiff wind rakes the water, swirls dead leaves and nods the tall brown cattails along the bank. Farther back in the woods it's very still, cypress trees and knees, thick vines, an abandoned beaver's lodge. Buzzards float overhead, black smudges against the gray clouds. Once, on this trestle, armed with only fishing rods, my brother Jeff and I heard a panther scream. It's a sound I've never forgotten, like a madwoman's shriek. After that, we brought guns when we came to fish. But today I'm unarmed, and the only noise is the groan and hiss of bulldozers and trucks on a new-cut logging road a quarter-mile away.

I left the south four years ago, when I was thirty, to go to graduate school in Fayetteville, Arkansas, where among transplanted Yankees and westerners I realized how lucky I was to have been raised here in these southern woods among poachers and storytellers. I know, of course, that most people consider Arkansas the south, but it's not *my* south. My south—the one I haven't been able to get out of my blood or my imagination, the south where these stories take place—is lower Alabama, lush and green and full of death, the wooded counties between the Alabama and Tombigbee Rivers.

1

Yesterday at five A.M. I left Fayetteville and drove seven hundred miles south to my parents' new house in Mobile, and this morning I woke early and drove two more hours, past the grit factory and the chemical plants where I worked in my twenties, to Dickinson, the community where we lived until I was eighteen. It's a tiny place, one store (now closed) and a post office in the same building, a kudzu-netted graveyard, railroad tracks. I've been finishing a novella that takes place in these woods—in the story, a man is killed right beneath where I'm standing—and I'm here looking for details of the landscape, for things I might've forgotten.

To get to the Blowout, I picked through a half-mile of pine trees that twelve years ago had been one of my family's cornfields. I hardly recognized the place. I walked another half-mile along the new logging road, then climbed onto the railroad track, deep woods on both sides, tall patchwork walls of briar and tree, brown thrashers hopping along unseen like something pacing me. My father and aunts and uncles used to own this land. It was ours. When my grandfather died, he divided almost six hundred acres among his five children. He expected them to keep it in the family, but one by one they sold it for logging or to hunting clubs. Today none of it is ours.

I'm about to leave when I notice that fifty yards down the track something big is disentangling itself from the trees. For a moment I reexperience the shock I used to feel whenever I saw a deer, but this is only a hunter. I see that he's spotted me, is climbing onto the tracks and coming this way. Because I lived in these parts for eighteen years, I expect to know him, and for a moment I feel foolish: What am I doing here at the Blowout, during hunting season, without a gun?

It's a familiar sensation, this snag of guilt, because when I was growing up, a boy who didn't hunt was branded as a pussy. For some reason, I never wanted to kill things, but I wasn't bold enough to say so. Instead, I did the expected: went to church on Sundays and on Wednesday nights, said "Yes ma'am" and "No sir" to my elders. And I hunted.

Though I hated (and still hate) to get up early, I rose at four A.M. Though I hated the cold, I made my way through the icy woods, climbing into one of our family's deer stands or sitting at the base of a thick live oak to still hunt, which simply means waiting for a buck to walk by so you can shoot him. And because I came to hunting for the wrong reasons, and because I worried that my father, brother and uncles might see through my ruse, I became the most zealous hunter of us all.

I was the one who woke first in the mornings and shook Jeff awake. The first in the truck. The first to the railroad track, where we climbed the rocky hill and crept toward the Blowout, our splitting-up point. On those mornings, the stars still out, it would be too dark to see our breath, the cross ties creaking beneath our boots, and I would walk the quietest, holding my double-barrel sixteen-gauge shotgun against my chest, my bare thumb on the safety and my left trigger finger on the first of its two triggers. When we got to the Blowout, I'd go left, without a word, and Jeff right. I'd creep down the loose rocks, every sound amplified in the still morning, and I'd step quietly over the frozen puddles below and into the dark trees.

In the woods, the stars disappeared overhead as if swiped away, and I inched forward with my hand before my face to feel for briars, my eyes watering from the cold. When I got far enough, I found a tree to sit beneath, shivering and miserable, thinking of the stories I wanted to write and hoping for something to shoot. Because at sixteen, I'd never killed a deer, which meant I was technically still a pussy.

Of course there were a lot of real hunters in my family, including my father. Though he no longer hunted, Gerald Franklin commanded the respect of the most seasoned woodsman because as a young man he'd been a legendary killer of turkeys (and we all knew that turkey hunters consider themselves the only serious sportsmen, disdaining deer or any other game the way fly fishermen look down on bait fishermen). Dad never bragged about the toms he'd shot, but we heard everything from our uncles. According to them, my father had been the wildest of us all, getting up earlier and staying in the woods later than any man in the county.

There's a story he tells where he woke on a spring Sunday to go hunting—he never used a clock, relying instead on his "built-in" alarm. Excited because he knew which tree a gobbler had roosted in the evening before, he dressed in the dark so he wouldn't wake my mother, pregnant with me. When he got to the woods it was still pitch black, so he settled down to wait for daylight. An hour passed, and no sign of light. Instead of going back home, though, he laid his gun aside, lit a cigarette and continued to wait for a dawn that wouldn't arrive for three more hours. Later, laughing, he told my uncles he'd gotten to the woods around one A.M.

But at some point, before I started first grade, he quit hunting. I always figured it was because he'd found religion. I grew up going to the Baptist church every Sunday with a father who was a deacon, not a hunter. Ours was a godly household—to this day

4

I've never heard Dad curse—and we said grace at every meal (even if we ate out) and prayed as a family each night, holding hands. After church on Sunday mornings, Dad sat in our living room and read his Bible, wearing his tie all day, then loaded us in the big white Chrysler to head back to church in the evening.

If we passed the three Wiggins brothers, dressed in old clothes and carrying hand-cut fishing poles, Dad shook his head and gave us all a minisermon on the perils of fishing on the Lord's day. Though neither he nor anyone else has ever confirmed it, I've always thought that by not hunting he was paying a kind of self-imposed penance for the Saturday nights in his youth he'd spent in pool halls, and for the Sundays he'd skipped church to chase turkeys.

Sometimes, in my own hunting years, huddled against a sweet gum, waiting for noon or dusk to give me permission to leave the woods, I'd imagine my father as a younger man, slipping through the trees, still wearing his blue mechanic's shirt with his name stitched across the chest, grease from his garage under his fingernails, carrying in his callused hands the same sixteen-gauge shotgun he would later give me. He was heading toward where he'd heard a gobbler that morning before work.

When he got to the spot, he knelt and, cradling the shotgun, removed from the pocket of his old army jacket the little box turkey caller he would give my brother years later. It was wooden and hollow like a tiny guitar box. You drew a peg over its green surface as gently as you could, the way you'd peel an apple without breaking the skin. If you knew what you were doing, it made a quiet, perfect hen's cluck, something a man could barely hear, but a sound that would snap a gobbler's head around half a mile away. After Dad had clucked a time or two, he waited, and when he heard the distant answer—that mysterious lovely cry, half a

5

rooster's crow and half the whinny of a horse—he worked his jaw like a man shifting his chewing tobacco, and from under his tongue he moved his "yepper" to the roof of his mouth.

Year after year, in our stockings for Christmas, he'd been giving Jeff and me our own yeppers, tiny plastic turkey callers the size of a big man's thumbnail, and he would try to teach us to "yep" the way turkeys do. Jeff caught on quickly, but it made me gag.

It was this kind of gift that let me know my father wanted me to hunt, though he never pressed, and let me know he was bothered by the fact that, until I was fifteen years old, I played with dolls. Not girls' dolls, but "action figures." The original G.I. Joe with his fuzzy crew cut and a scar on his chin, Johnny West with his painted-on clothes, Big Jim with his patented karate chop: I had them all. I loved playing with them, and because Jeff was two years younger than I was, he did whatever I did. But while he would wrench off G.I. Joe's head and hands to examine how the doll was put together, I would imagine that my G.I. Joe was Tarzan of the Apes. One of my sister's Barbie dolls, stripped to a skimpy jungle bikini, became Jane. A foot-tall Chewbacca was Kerchak, an ape. In the lush green summer afternoons, Jeff and I built African villages out of sticks and vines. We dug a wide trench across our backyard and with the garden hose made a muddy brown river filled with rubber snakes and plastic crocodiles.

When the Wiggins brothers pedaled up on their rusty bicycles—they were stringy, sun-yellowed boys who smelled like sweat and fish and never wore shirts or shoes in summer, who lived a mile away down a dirt road in the woods—Jeff and I would toss our dolls into the bushes and pretend to be cleaning up a mess in the backyard.

"Wanna go fishin'?" Kent Wiggins would ask, stuffing his

lower lip with Skoal. His father worked for the lumber mill, and
Kent would get a job there when he turned eighteen. I envied
them the ease with which they accepted and handled their lives,
the way they spit between their teeth, flicked a rod, fired a rifle.

Jeff and I always went wherever they asked us to go—I was
afraid of being laughed at and being called a mama's boy for
saying no, and Jeff enjoyed the fishing. And sitting on the trestle
over the Blowout, watching the Wigginses and my little brother
pull in catfish after catfish, I'd long for my G.I. Joe, and hate the
longing.

Once, when I was newly fifteen in Kmart with ten birthday
dollars to spend, Dad came up beside me.

"You could buy a hunting knife," he whispered.

"Gerald . . ." my mother warned.

He let go of my shoulders, put his hands in his pockets.

"He wants to get a new outfit for his G.I. Joe," Mom said to
Dad.

I'd never felt more like a pussy.

So the hell with it, I thought, and headed for the tall line of
fishing rods I could see beyond the toy aisle. Dad fell into step
beside me. He let me shave the bristly hairs off his wrist in search
of the sharpest knife while Mom stood with her arms folded near
the stink bait, glaring into space. At the checkout counter, I
watched Dad add another five to my ten dollars for the Old Timer
Sharpfinger I'd picked. When we left the store, he had his arm
around me.

As Dad drove us home, I asked him if he wished I didn't play
with G.I. Joes. Mom sat far across the long seat, looking out her
window. At my question, her head jerked toward Dad, who

stopped whistling. He glanced at her before catching my eye in the rearview mirror.

"No," he said. "I'm real proud of you, son. I'm glad you've got . . . imagination."

When Jeff killed his first buck, a spike, I was there.

Despite being younger, Jeff has always been a much better shot than I am. I'd gotten Dad's sixteen-gauge at Christmas, but Jeff had unwrapped a Marlin thirty-thirty lever-action rifle. The fact that I was eighteen and still using a shotgun didn't go unnoticed—the boy with the weakest aim always gets the scattergun because its spray of buckshot gives more chances for a hit than a single bullet. Never mind that my sixteen-gauge was an antique that had belonged to my grandfather, a rare Foxboro crafted of blued Sterlingworth steel, a side-by-side model that broke open behind the walnut stock. The shells slid in and the breech closed with a muffled snap, a sound more like cloth than metal. It's a gun I can take apart—barrel, forearm, stock—and reassemble in thirty seconds. A gun worth over two thousand dollars. Yet in the woods, I was ashamed of it.

The high school closed on opening day of deer season, and on that first morning in 1980, Jeff and I sat in opposite tree stands—small seats built overlooking a wide field where deer came to graze—and from mine I watched my brother sight me with the scope of his rifle. I sat rigid, silent, ready for a deer, while a hundred yards away, Jeff waved at me. Gave me the finger. He pissed from off his stand, *twice*. He yawned. Slept. But as one hour became two, I stayed stock-still—I didn't have Jeff's instinct for knowing when to be ready, for being relaxed until it was time to raise your gun and aim. My limbs began to tingle, the blood slowing in my veins like a creek icing up. I didn't blink for so long that the woods blurred, and I began to feel that I was part of them, the trees and the leaves taking on a buzzing resonance and losing their sharp edges, the buzzing increasing like a hornet loose inside my head, and for an instant I hung there, the center of something, seeing from my ears, hearing from my eyes, the world around me a tangible glow of brindle noise. Then I blinked.

And from across the field came Jeff's gunshot.

From then on, I insisted on sitting in Jeff's lucky stand. A year later, early in the 1981 season, the sixteen-gauge in my lap, I was there, waiting. Tense. It was dusk, and I was losing hope again. I'd been hunting like a fanatic—once or twice a day. I'd stopped taking books with me. I'd seen deer and even missed a doe, the fabled buck fever claiming me with violent seizures, my gun barrel shaking, teeth clacking.

Now, on the lucky stand, I didn't see the deer when it walked into the field. You seldom do: they just appear. And if it's a buck, like this one, you notice the antlers first, the sleekest, sharpest things in the world, not bone but blood vessels dried and hard as stone. On the stand, I lifted the jittering shotgun, slowly, thumbing the safety, the buck less than twenty yards from where I sat trembling.

I aimed, blood roaring in my ears, and fired, not feeling the kick.

The buck raised his head, still chewing. His antlers seemed to unwind as he looked around, wondering where that blast had come from. At some point, I remembered that I had another barrel, and I began pulling the trigger again, before finally real- izing that I had to pull the *second* trigger. When I fired, the deer buckled and recovered, then vanished, replaced by the noise of something tearing through the dead leaves behind me, a painful sound hacking down the gully.

From across the field, Jeff's voice: "Kill anything?"

I descended the ladder, my hands shaking. At the bottom, I struggled to break open the gun, and shells from my pocket fell to the ground. I reloaded, and, nearly crying, slid to the bottom of the gully.

The deer—thank God—was there. Still alive, but down. His side caving in and out and a hind leg quivering. Approaching him, I counted his points—six, seven, eight—an eight-point! What I was supposed to do now, what Dad and my uncles had drilled into me, was to cautiously approach the buck, draw my knife and cut his throat, watch him bleed to death. But in my excitement, I forgot this. Instead, I moved to within three feet of the deer's flagging side and flipped the sixteen-gauge's safety off. I put a finger on each of the shotgun's triggers, and, holding the gun at my hip, pulled them at the same time.

That night, my entire family admired the deer lying in the back of Dad's pickup, its black eyes turning foggy. It's traditional to rub blood on a boy's face when he kills his first deer, but Dad had a lesson to teach. I'd gut-shot the buck so badly that a lot of meat had been ruined. The hole I'd blown in his side was big enough to put my head in, and Dad came up behind me and did exactly that. When he pulled me out by my neck, I was almost sick, but I managed to hold it, like a man. That was when everyone gathered around me, my uncles and Jeff clapping my back, Mom and my aunts hugging me, trying not to get blood on their blouses.

When I tell this story, I end by saying that nothing except Beth Ann accepting my marriage proposal on a warm wine-and-cheese afternoon in Paris has surpassed the feeling I had that night. As Dad guided me through cleaning the deer, peeling down its skin, trimming away the small white pockets of fat, my eight-year-old cousin approached us. When the boy saw the buck's bloody, empty body cavity, he tumbled away, gagging. Dad rolled his eyes at me. Then we began to quarter the red meat, my face and neck still bloody, my hair stiff with gore.

Near the close of the same season, I sat on a wooded hill in a plot of land on which my father, when he sold it, had been wise enough to retain the mineral and hunting rights. It was only two months after I'd killed my eight-point, but now things were different because Jeff had bragged about the buck at school. Whenever I told the story, I always made myself seem foolish by giving the deer both barrels at such close range. People seemed to like that. I was discovering the power of self-depreciation and didn't mind being laughed at as long as everyone knew I'd killed the deer. And they did: Coach Horn had led me to his office behind the gym and shown me the antlers on his walls. For the first time in my life, I wasn't a pussy. No. Sitting on the hillside that evening, I was a man who'd enjoyed his first taste of blood and who wanted more.

It was a mild January day, the leaves crisp, stirred by the wind to an almost constant rustle. Suddenly, an even bigger eight-point buck had materialized at the bottom of the ravine, stealing among the live oaks. First I saw his rack of antlers as he nosed along the ground, eating acorns. Then his shoulders. His flat tail. The color of dead leaves, he blended so well into the hillside that I only saw him when he moved. My heart began to rattle, and, as if he heard it, the buck raised his head and looked right at me. He lifted his nose and snorted, his nostrils gleaming. For a moment he seemed to vanish, to have never been there, but before I could panic I saw him again as he took a step away from me.

Somehow, I did everything right—aimed when he put his head down, squeezed instead of jerked the trigger—and *still* damn near missed. My buckshot pellets sprayed the deer across his neck, face and antlers, chipping them, bringing bloody beads across his cheeks, putting out one eye and—we saw this later—injuring his spine so that he only had use of his front legs, the back two paralyzed. I stood and watched him drag himself through the leaves, trying to get away, pawing and stumbling down the gully-side.

From the next hollow over, Jeff called, "Kill anything?"

I half fell to the bottom of the ravine. The deer lay still, just a slight rippling of his big leathery sides, blood glistening on his black nose. While I circled him, gun ready, he watched me, his head up, turning to keep me in sight. One eye was red and bleeding, but the other remained bright and clear. From over the hill, I heard Jeff crashing through the leaves. I knew he'd heard my shot—my single shot—and I didn't want him to hear another.

Why didn't I cut the deer's throat? There was no shame in that, and it was the safest way to avoid the buck's deadly antlers. But instead I did something that shocks me to this day. I dropped the sixteen-gauge and drew my Sharpfinger. I approached the deer, watching him follow me with his good eye. Carefully, the way you'd reach to pin a snake with your foot, I stuck out my leg and put my boot on the buck's neck, forcing his head down. I knelt on top of him, straddled his back. Now I heard his ragged breathing, felt his heat on my thighs. I took one thick tine of his antlers in my right hand and turned his good eye away so he couldn't see. He didn't resist. I raised the knife and began to stab him in the shoulder where I knew his heart was. The buck barely moved beneath me, and the blade cut cleanly, as if I were sticking soft dirt. I stabbed him twelve times, in what I thought a buckshot pattern would be. Then I laid my hand on the deer's hot shoulder, over the wounds I'd made, and felt that his heart had stopped.

By the time Jeff came running down the hill, I'd begun my first solo act of field dressing. It was—and still is—the biggest buck anyone in my family had killed, weighing over 220, seventy pounds more than I weighed at the time.

Later, as we hoisted the deer up beneath our skinning tree, Dad noticed the holes in the buck's side. He nodded to Jeff and me. "Now boys," he said, "*that* was a good shot." With my knife, I made a series of cuts along the deer's hind legs, and Jeff and Dad helped me peel down the buck's fur—a noise like Velcro makes—to reveal the nearly purple carcass beneath.

Night had fallen, and with a flashlight Dad looked at the deer's side. He bent, examining it more closely, working his finger into one of the knife slits. Then he stared me down.

"Son," he said, "is that what I think it is?"

I didn't answer.

He reached for the deer's head and lifted it by the giant, chipped, eight-point rack, a set of antlers so big I could step into it like pants. He grabbed me by the small of my back and jammed me into my dead deer. He brought the antlers against my stomach and pushed the points in so hard they hurt.

"Do you know what 'eviscerate' means?" he asked me.

Now, at the Blowout, the hunter approaches me on the trestle. I expect it's one of the Wiggins brothers, and here I am again, as gunless and guilty and foolish as if I'm holding a doll. But as the man draws closer, a scoped rifle in the crook of his arm, I see from his expensive camouflage, fluorescent orange hat and face paint that he's not from around here. The men who live in these parts hunt in work clothes, old boots and faded camo jackets passed down from their fathers or grandfathers. They would never wear face paint or an orange hat. When I hunted I used to carry such a cap in my pocket in case I ran into a game warden, but most of the hunters I grew up admiring simply never ran into game wardens. These men raise their own coon and squirrel dogs. Their rifles have taped stocks. Although they often kill out of season or at night, they usually eat what they kill. I admire them, and so I feel a flicker of distaste for this outsider.

"Hello," I say to the fellow, probably a lawyer from Mobile. "Kill anything?"

"Get out of here," he says.

I cock my head. "I'm sorry?"

"You heard me. This is private property. You're trespassing on our hunting club." He swings his gun barrel toward the woods on the right, as if pointing to his buddies lurking in the shadows, their faces green and black, twigs in their hair, expensive rifles aimed at my head.

I spit through my teeth. I don't tell him that this used to be my family's land, that I've dragged deer over this very track, spent hours on this goddamn trestle. Instead I say, "The railroad's not private property."

"The hell it's not," he says. And raises the rifle, aims at me.

We stand facing one another. It will be dark soon, and from the left side of the track comes the distant snarl of a logger's power saw. I try to see myself through the hunter's eyes: my ragged jeans, my leather jacket and hiking boots. To him I probably look like a hippie, like the last thing you'd expect to find out here.

Meanwhile, the hunter is edgy, glancing behind him in the woods. "I'm not gonna tell you again," he says.

The saw rattles to a stop, then revs up again.

"You hear that?" I ask. "That'll ruin your hunting more than I will."

I know I should leave, but instead I sit on the cold rail and look away from the hunter, at the woods. I recall a story my father told me. He was turkey hunting down here early on a Sunday morning. Creeping along, he heard a wavering voice, and it spooked him. He followed it through the trees until, in the distance, he saw an old black preacher standing on a stump, practicing his sermon. He had a giant white Bible in one hand and a red handkerchief for face-mopping in the other. Despite the forty-degree weather, his shirtsleeves were rolled up. Dad stopped and listened to the man's tremulous voice, knowing that every turkey for miles was gone, that his hunting was spoiled. He might as well have gone home. When I asked him if he was angry he said no, just spooked.

I turn and look at the hunter's camouflaged face. "You ever hunt turkeys?"

"Go to hell," he says, and walks away. He doesn't look back, just heads into the woods. When he's gone I stand up and close my coat. Take a last long look at the Blowout, then make my way carefully down the side of the tracks. I duck under the darkening magnolia branches on the other side and start back toward the logging road.

I know, as I walk, that I'm not the fancy-rifled lawyer in face paint and new camouflage, yet neither am I the dedicated native hunter I pretended to be all those years. Now when I return here, to Dickinson, it's as a kind of stranger—after all, I've left, gotten educated, lost some of my drawl. I even married a Yankee. And coming back like this to hunt for details for my stories feels a bit like poaching on land that used to be mine. But I've never lost the need to tell of my Alabama, to reveal it, lush and green and full of death. So I return, knowing what I've learned. I come back, where life is slow dying, and I poach for stories. I poach because I want to recover the paths while there's still time, before the last logging trucks rumble through and the old, dark ways are at last forever hewn.

grit

Chugging and clanging among the dark pine trees north of Mobile, Alabama, the Black Beauty Minerals plant was a rickety green hull of storage tanks, chutes and conveyor belts. Glen, the manager, felt like the captain of a ragtag spaceship that had crash-landed, a prison barge full of poachers and thieves, smugglers and assassins.

The owners, Ernie and Dwight, lived far away, in Detroit, and when the Black Beauty lost its biggest client—Ingalls Shipbuilding—to government budget cuts, they ordered Glen to lay off his two-man night shift. One of the workers was a long-haired turd Glen enjoyed letting go, a punk who would've likely failed his next drug test. But the other man, Roy Jones, did some bookmaking on the side, and Glen had been in a betting slump lately. So when Roy, who'd had a great year as a bookie, crunched over the gritty black yard to the office, Glen owed him over four thousand dollars.

Roy, a fat black man, strode in without knocking and wedged himself into the chair across from Glen's desk, probably expecting more stalling of the debt.

Glen cleared his throat. "I've got some bad news, Roy—"

"Chill, baby," Roy said. He removed his hard hat, which left its imprint in his hair. "I know I'm fixing to get laid off, and I

17

got a counteroffer for you." He slid a cigar from his hat lining and smelled it.

Glen was surprised. The Ingalls announcement hadn't come until a few hours ago. Ernie and Dwight had just released him from their third conference call of the afternoon, the kind where they both yelled at him at the same time.

"How'd you find that out, Roy?" he asked.

Roy lit his cigar. "One thing you ain't learned yet is how to get the system doggie-style. Two of my associates work over at Ingalls, and one of 'em been fucking the bigwig's secretary."

"Well—"

"Hang on, Glen. I expect E and D done called you and told you to lay my big fat ass off. But that's cool, baby." He tipped his ashes into his hard hat. " 'Cause I got other irons in the fire."

He said he had an "independent buyer" for some Black Beauty sandblasting grit. Said he had, in fact, a few lined up. What he wanted was to run an off-the-books night shift for a few hours a night, three nights a week. He said he had an associate who'd deliver the stuff. The day-shifters could be bought off. Glen could doctor the paperwork so the little production wouldn't be noticed by Ernie and Dwight.

"But don't answer now," Roy said, replacing his hard hat. "Sleep on it tonight, baby. Mull it over."

Glen—a forty-two-year-old, ulcer-ridden, insomniac, half-alcoholic chronic gambler—mulled Roy's idea over in his tiny apartment that evening by drinking three six-packs of Bud Light. He picked up the phone and placed a large bet with Roy on the upcoming Braves–Giants game, taking San Francisco because Barry Bonds was on fire. Then he dialed the number of the Pizza

poachers

Hut managed by his most recent ex-wife's new boyfriend, placed an order for five extra-large thick-crust pies with pineapple and double anchovies, and had it delivered to another of his ex-wives' houses for her and her boyfriend. Glen had four ex-wives in all, and he was still in love with each of them. Every night as he got drunk it felt like somebody had shot him in the chest with buckshot and left four big airy holes in his heart, holes that grew with each beer, as if—there was no other way he could think of it— his heart were being sandblasted.

The Braves rallied in the eighth and Bonds's sixteen-game hitting streak was snapped, so when Roy came by the next day, Glen owed him another eight hundred dollars and change.

Roy sat down. "You made up your mind yet?"

"Impossible," Glen said. "Even if I wanted to, I couldn't go along. Ernie and Dwight'd pop in out of nowhere and we'd all be up the creek."

Today Roy wore tan slacks and a brown silk shirt. Shiny brown shoes and, when he crossed his legs, thin argyle socks. A brown fedora in his lap. The first time Glen had seen him in anything but work clothes.

Roy shook a cigar from its box and lit it. "Glen, you the most gullible motherfucker ever wore a hard hat. Don't you reckon I know when them tight-asses is coming down here?"

"How? Got somebody fucking their wives?"

Roy hesitated. "My cousin's daughter work in the Detroit airport."

Glen's mind flashed a quick slideshow of Ernie and Dwight's past disastrous visits. "You might've mentioned that four years ago."

"Baby," Roy said, "I'll cut you in for ten percent of every load we sell."

"There's a recession, Roy. I can't unload this grit to save my life, and if I can't, you sure as hell can't."

Roy chuckled. "Got-damn, boy." He pulled out a wad of hundred-dollar bills. "This is what I done presold. I got friends all up and down the coast. They got some rusty-ass shit needs sandblasting. You ain't no salesman, Glen. You couldn't sell a whore on a battleship."

"Roy, it's illegal."

"Go look out yonder." Roy pointed to the window overlooking the black-grit parking lot.

Glen obeyed. A big white guy with a little head was leaning against Roy's cream-colored El Dorado, carving at his fingernails with a long knife.

"That's my associate, Snakebite," Roy said. "He'll be delivering the stuff. He also collect for me, if you know what I mean."

Glen knew.

"Up till now," Roy said, "you been getting off easy 'cause you was the boss. Now that that's changed . . ."

Glen looked at him. "You threatening me, Roy?"

"Naw, baby. I'm a businessman." Roy took out his pocket ledger. "As of now, I'm forgetting every got-damn cent you owe me." Glen watched Roy write *paid* by the frighteningly high red figure he would've been having nightmares about, had he been able to sleep.

Roy started running his phantom night shift Monday through Wednesday nights. To keep the four day-shifters quiet, he gave them a slight payoff—a "taste"—each week. So they clocked in in the mornings and pretended the machinery wasn't hot, that the plant hadn't run all night. And Glen, hungover, took his clipboard and measuring tape out and stared at the dwindling stockpiles of raw grit where Roy had taken material. Then he went back across the yard into his office, locked the door, rubbed his eyes, doctored his paperwork and—some days—threw up.

Staring out the window, he worried that the day shift would rat to Ernie and Dwight. He'd never been close to the workers— in his first week as manager, four years before, he'd confiscated the radio they kept in the control room. Instead of spending afternoons in his office making sales calls the way the previous manager had, Glen had stayed out in the heat with the men, cracking the whip, having the plant operator retake grit samples, watching the millwright repair leaks, making sure the payloader's fittings were well-greased. He timed the guys' breaks, stomped into the break room if they stayed a minute past their half hour. If someone got a personal phone call, Glen would go to another extension and pick up and say, "Excuse me," in an icy tone and wait for them to hang up.

In the plant, they were supposed to wear hard hats, safety glasses, steel-toe boots, leather gloves, earplugs and, depending on where they worked, a dust mask or respirator. Glen struck here, too, because his predecessor had let the guys grow lax. In those first months, Glen had stepped on their toes to check for steel and yelled in their ears to check for plugs. He'd written them up for the tiniest safety violation and put it in their permanent files.

So they hated him. They took orders sullenly and drew a finger across their throats as a warning signal when he approached. They never invited him to participate in their betting pools or asked him to get a beer after work.

Now Glen swore to give up gambling. He locked himself in

the office during the day and made halfhearted sales calls: "The unique thing about our sandblasting grit," he'd say wearily, "is that no piece, no matter how small, has a round edge." At night, he stayed home and watched sitcoms and nature shows instead of baseball. When cabin fever struck, he went to the movies instead of the dog track or the casino boats in Biloxi. He even managed to curb his drinking on weeknights.

Until early July. There was an Independence Day weekend series between Atlanta and the Cards in St. Louis and the plant had a four-day weekend. A drunk Glen, who when lonely sometimes called 1-900 handicapping lines, got a great tip from Lucky Dave Rizetti—"A sure by-God thing," Lucky Dave promised. "Take the Bravos, take 'em for big money." And Glen took them, betting almost two grand over the four games. But the series was filled with freaky incidents, relief pitchers hitting home runs, Golden-Glovers making stupid two-base throwing errors, etc.

So on Tuesday, the holiday over, Glen was back in debt. Then add the fact that the lawyers of exes two and three had been sending letters threatening lawsuits if Glen didn't pay his alimony. The lawyers said they'd get a court order and garnish his wages. Christ, if Ernie and Dwight got wind of that, they'd fly down and can him for sure.

They came twice a year or so, the old bastards, for spot inspections, speaking in their Yankee accents and wearing polished hard hats on their prim gray crew cuts. They would fly in from Detroit, first class, and rent a Caddy and get suites at the top of the Riverview downtown. They'd bring rolled-up plans to the plant and walk around frowning and making notes. Glen always felt ill when they were on-site—they constantly grumbled about lack of production or low sales figures or how an elevator wasn't up to spec. They'd peer into his red eyes and sniff his breath. He would follow them around the plant's perimeter, his chin nicked from shaving, and he'd nod and hold his stomach.

On Tuesday, after Independence Day, Glen sat in his office staring at the electric bill—he would have to account for the extra power the phantom night shift was using—when Roy stuck his head in the door. He smiled, smoking a cigar, and sat down across from Glen's desk.

"Just come by to tell you we fixing to start running four nights a week," Roy said.

Glen started to object, but there was a shrill noise.

"Hang on." Roy brought a slim cellular phone out of his pocket.

Glen shrugged and doodled (man dangling by noose) on his desk calendar while Roy took another order for grit.

When Roy snapped the phone shut, Glen said, "No. You can't go to four nights. Who the hell was that? They want *two* loads? Never mind. Your night shift's gotta stop altogether, end of story."

"Impossible," Roy said.

"Impossible?"

"Look out the window."

Glen obeyed, saw a cute young woman in Roy's car. She was frowning.

"You see that pretty little thing?" Roy asked. "You know how old she is? Nineteen, Glen. *Nineteen.* She the freshest thing in the world, too. She go jogging every morning, and when she come back she don't even smell bad. Her breath don't stink in the morning." Roy coughed. "I wake up my breath smell like burnt tar."

"Roy—"

"You think a fresh little girl like that's with me 'cause she love me? Hell no. She with me 'cause I'm getting rich. So no, baby, we can't stop. Business just too damn good. Which remind me—" He opened his ledger. "You back up in four figures again."

"Roy, just stick to the subject at hand. I'm not asking you to stop. I'm ordering you to stop."

"Baby," Roy said quietly, "you ain't exactly in a strong bargaining position. Who's E and D gonna hold responsible if they hear about our little operation? You the manager. You the one been falsifying records. Naw, baby. The 'subject' ain't whether or not old Roy's gonna stop making grit. The 'subject' is what to do about all that money you owe me."

What they did was compromise. Roy said he'd been too busy to make grit and look after his bookmaking business. So Glen would go to work for him, at night. Roy would forget about the two grand and pay Glen ten bucks an hour to work nine hours a night, four nights a week.

"I bet you can use the extra bread," Roy said. "That alimony can eat a man up."

Then Roy said he needed Glen's office; the phones were better. It was quieter, he said. He could think. So that night Glen worked in the plant and Roy used the air-conditioned office. Sweating under the tanks, Glen saw Roy's fat silhouette behind the curtains, and he uncapped his flask and toasted the irony. He spent the night in the hot, claustrophobic control room, watching gauges, adjusting dials and taking samples; climbing into the front end loader once an hour and filling the hopper with raw material; on top of the tanks measuring the amount of grit they'd made; and standing by the loading chute, filling Snakebite's big purple Peterbilt.

At six that morning, with the plant shut down and Roy gone, Glen slogged to the office before the day-shifters clocked in. The room smelled like cigars, and Glen made a mental note to start smoking them in case Ernie and Dwight popped in. He locked the door behind him and pulled off his shoes and poured out little piles of grit. He lay back on his desk, exhausted, put his hands over his face, shut his eyes, and got his first good sleep in months.

Snakebite, six foot five, also slept during the day, in his Peterbilt, in the cab behind the seat, the truck parked among the pines near the plant. He showered every other day in the break room and ate canned pork and beans and Vienna sausages that he speared with his pocketknife. He had a tattoo on his left biceps, a big diamondback rattler with its mouth opened, tongue and fangs extended. He wore pointed snakeskin cowboy boots but no cowboy hat because adult hat sizes swallowed his tiny head. To Glen, he looked like a football player wearing shoulder pads but no helmet. He said he "hailed" from El Paso, Texas, but he'd "vamoosed" because his wife, a "mean little filly" who'd once stabbed him, had discovered that he was "stepping out" with a waitress in Amarillo.

Glen knew this and much more because Snakebite never stopped talking. One night, as the truck loaded, Snakebite showed Glen a rare World War I trench knife, a heavy steel blade with brass knuckles for a handle.

"I collect knives," Snakebite said. "Looky here." He bent and pulled up a tight jeans leg over his boot, revealing a white-handled stiletto.

"My Mississippi Gambler," Snakebite said. "It's a throwing

25

knife. See this quick unhitching gadget on the holster?" He
flipped a snap and the knife came right out of his boot into his
hand. "This is the one my wife stabbed me with," he said. He
showed Glen the scar, a white line on his left forearm. Glen didn't
have any scars from his ex-wives that he could show, so he uncapped his flask and knocked back a swig. He offered the flask
to Snakebite, who took it.

"Don't mind if I do, Slick," he said, winking.

"Where's this load going?" Glen asked, nodding toward the
black stream of grit falling into the truck. He'd been curious
about Roy's clients, thinking he might try to steal the business.

Snakebite grinned and punched him in the shoulder. "Shit,
boy. You oughta know that's classified. You find out old Roy's
secrets and he's outta business. Then I'm outta business."

"So." Glen swallowed. "I hear you do a little, um, collecting
for Roy."

Snakebite drained the flask. "Don't worry about that, Slick.
Old Roy ain't never sicced me on anybody I liked. And even if
he did, hell, it ain't ever as bad as you see in the movies."

Working nights for Roy Jones Grit, Inc., Glen wore a ratty
T-shirt, old sneakers, a Braves cap and short pants. He turned off
every breaker and light he could spare to keep the electric bill
low, so the place was dark and dangerous. He began carrying a
flashlight hooked to his belt. He tried to cut power during the
day, too. He adjusted all the electrical and mechanical equipment
to their most efficient settings. He even turned the temperature
dial in the break-room refrigerator to "warmer" and stole the
microwave (supposedly a great wattage-drainer) from its shelf and
pawned it, then called the day-shifters in for a meeting where he

gave the "thief" a chance to confess. No one did, and the meeting became a lecture where Glen urged the men to "conserve energy, not just for the good of the plant, but for the sake of the whole fucking environment." To set an example, he told them, he would stop using the air conditioner in the office.

But not Roy: Roy ran the AC full-blast all night so that the office was ice-cold. Not that Glen had a lot of time to notice. Typically it took one man to operate the plant and another the loader. Doing both, as well as loading Snakebite's truck, Glen found himself run ragged by morning, so covered with sweat, grit and dust that the lines in his face and the corners of his eyes and the insides of his ears were black, and his snot, when he blew his nose, even that was black.

One evening in mid-July Glen trudged to the office to complain. He opened the door and came face-to-face with the young woman from Roy's car. She had lovely black skin and round brown eyes. Rich dark hair in cornrow braids that would've hung down except for her headband. She wore bright green spandex pants and a sports bra.

"Hello," Glen said.

"Right." She flounced into the bathroom.

Glen hurried to Roy's desk. "What the hell's she doing here?"

Roy had his feet and a portable television on the desk. He was watching the Yankees. "Your new assistant," he said. "You just keep your got-damn hands off her."

"She can't work here." Glen glanced at the TV. "What's the score? What if she gets hurt? She's just a girl."

"Woman," she said from the door.

"Tied up," Roy said.

27

"Sorry," Glen said. "Miss . . . ?"

"Ms."

Roy cranked the volume without looking at them. "You been whining about having too much work every night," he told Glen, "so Jalalieh gonna start driving the loader for you."

Jalalieh.

Ja-LA-lee-ay.

As Glen instructed her in the operation of the Caterpillar 950 front-end loader, she stayed quiet. It was crowded in the cab and he had to hang on the stepladder to allow her room to work the levers that raised, lowered and swiveled the bucket. She smelled good, even over the diesel odor of the payloader, and he soon found himself staring at her thighs and biceps.

"You work out a lot?" he asked.

"Careful big bad Roy don't see you making small talk," she said.

"Pull back on the bucket easy," he said. "You'll spill less."

"That's better, little man. Keep it professional."

So with great patience and fear he instructed her on how to gain speed when heading in to scoop raw material, how to drop the bucket along the ground and dig from the bottom of a pile, locking the raise lever and working the swivel lever back and forth as it rose to get the fullest bucket. He showed her how to hold a loaded bucket high and peer beneath it to see, how to roll smoothly over the rough black ground and up the ramp behind the plant to the hopper. How to dump the bucket while shifting into reverse so the material fell evenly onto the hopper grate, and how to back down the ramp while lowering the bucket. She caught on quickly and within a few nights was a much better loader operator than most of the day shift guys. Glen watched from the ground with pride as she tore giant bulging bucketfuls from the piles and carried them safely over the yard. And as he noticed the way her breasts bounced when she passed, he felt the hot, gritty wind swirling and whistling through the caves of his heart.

A few nights later, while Glen and Snakebite watched the truck load, Snakebite explained about his tiny head.

"Everybody on my daddy's side's got little bitty heads," he said. "It's kinda like our trademark. We ain't got no butts, either. Look." He turned and, sure enough, there was all this spare material in the seat of his blue jeans. Snakebite laughed. "But me, I make up for it with my dick."

"Pardon?" Glen said.

"Well, I ain't fixing to whip it out, but I got the biggest durn cock-a-doodle-doo you liable to see on a white man. Yes sir," he said, lowering his voice so it was hard to hear over the roar of the plant, "when I get a hard-on, I ain't got enough loose skin left to close my eyes."

Glen, whose penis was average, took out his flask. He was unscrewing the lid when Jalalieh thundered past in the loader. When Glen glanced at Snakebite, the truck driver was looking after her with his eyes wide open.

The next night, as the truck loaded, something clattered behind them. Glen unclipped his flashlight and Snakebite followed him around a dark corner to the garbage cans. An armadillo had gotten into the trash, one of its feet in an aluminum pie-plate.

"Well, hello there, you old armored dildo," Snakebite said. When it tried to dart away, he cornered it. "Tell you what,

Slick"—he winked at Glen—"you keep a eye on our friend and I'll be right back."

He trotted toward his truck and Glen kept the flashlight aimed at the armadillo—gray, the size of a football, just squatting there, white icing on its snout. Soon Snakebite reappeared with a briefcase. He set it on a garbage can and opened it and rummaged around, finally coming out with something bundled in a towel. He unwrapped it and Glen saw several different-colored knives.

Snakebite grinned. "I bought 'em off a circus Indian chief used to chuck 'em at a squaw that spun on a big old wagon wheel."

He took a knife by its wide blade and flicked it. The armadillo jumped straight up and landed running, the handle poking out of its side. Snakebite fired another knife which ricocheted off the armadillo's back. Another stuck in its shoulder. A fourth knife bounced off the concrete. Glen glanced away, ashamed for not stopping Snakebite. When he looked again the armadillo lay on its side, inflating and deflating with loud rasps.

"I hate them sum-bitches," Snakebite said. He stepped forward and drew back his foot to punt the armadillo.

Suddenly a light flared, catching the two men like the headlights of night hunters: Jalalieh, in the loader, bore down on them, the bucket scraping the ground, igniting sparks. Glen dove one way and Snakebite the other as she plowed in like a freight train, sweeping up the armadillo, the garbage cans, the knives. In a second she was gone, disappearing around the plant, leaving them flat on their bellies with their heads covered like survivors of an explosion.

"That's a hot little honey," Snakebite said once he was back on his feet. He dusted off his jeans. "You reckon old Roy'd sell me a piece of that? Add it to my bill?"

It wasn't Glen's jealousy that surprised him. "You owe Roy money?"

"Yep. Borrowed it to get my truck painted."

"Roy's a loan shark too?"

"You ever see *Jaws*?" Snakebite asked.

Glen said he had.

"How 'bout *The Godfather*?"

"Yeah."

"Well, if Michael Corleone waded out in the ocean and fucked that shark, then you'd have old Roy."

Later, as Jalalieh climbed out of the loader, Glen stood waiting in the shadows.

"A what?"

"Tour," he repeated. "See, the Black Beauty, it's a state-of-the-art facility."

"This dump?"

"With cutting-edge technology." He grinned. "Get it?"

She folded her arms.

"Okay," Glen said. "The unique thing about our grit is that no piece—"

"Has a round edge. So what?"

Nevertheless, she allowed Glen to lead her around the plant, explaining how the raw material from the loader fell onto a conveyor belt, then into a machine similar to a grain elevator. From there it rode up into the dryer, a tall cylindrical oven which used natural gas to burn the moisture out. Next, the dry grit flowed into the crusher, a wide centrifuge that spun the grit at high speeds and smashed the grains against iron walls, pulverizing any outsized rock into smaller pieces. Finally, atop the plant, Glen showed her the shaker, a jingling, vibrating box the size of a coffin. Raising his voice to be heard, he explained how the shaker housed several screens and sifted the grit down through them, distributing it by size into the storage tanks under their feet.

Staring at the shaker, Jalalieh said, "It's like one of those motel beds you put a quarter in."

Every night and day the dryer dried and the crusher crushed and the shaker shook, sifting grit down through the screens into their proper tanks. To keep pieces from clogging the screens, rubber balls were placed between the layers when the screens were built. Little by little, the grit eroded the balls, so they'd gradually be whittled from the size of handballs down to marbles, then BBs, and finally they'd just disappear so that, every two weeks or so, Glen's day-shift guys would have to build new screens, add new balls. Since Glen had begun sleeping during the day, the workers had gotten lax again. While the grit clogged the shaker and gnawed holes in chutes and pipes and elevators and accumulated in piles that grew each hour, the day shift played poker in the control room, sunbathed on top of the tanks, had king-of-the-mountain contests on the stockpiles.

One morning, Glen was snoring on his desk when he heard something thump against the side of the office.

He rolled over, rubbing his eyes, squinting in the bright light, and he looked out the window at the plant shimmering against the hot white sky. Then he saw his entire four-man day crew and some tall guy playing baseball with an old shovel handle. There was a pitcher on a mound of grit with a box of the rubber screen balls open beside him. There were two fielders trying to shag the flies. There was a catcher wearing a respirator, hard hat and welding sleeves for protection. The batter was Snakebite, and he was whacking the pitched balls clear over the mountains of grit, nearly to the interstate.

Glen closed his eyes and went back to sleep.

Every night Glen scaled that ladder up between the storage tanks—quite a climb in the dark, over a hundred feet with no protection against gravity but the metal cage around the ladder. At the top, catwalks joined the tanks. Out past the handrails, darkness stretched all around, and in the distance blinked the lights of radio towers and chemical-plant smokestacks. The Black Beauty had its own blinking yellow beacon on a pole high above, a warning to low-flying aircraft, the one light Glen feared shutting off—certainly that would be illegal. It blinked every few seconds, illuminating the dusty air, and Glen followed his flashlight beam from tank to tank, prying open the heavy metal lids and unspooling over each an ancient measuring tape with a big iron bolt on its end.

A few nights after Jalalieh's tour, Glen climbed the ladder to take measurements. It was nearly dawn, and he'd just finished when he saw her. Hugging her knees, Jalalieh sat overhead, atop the tallest elevator platform, appearing and vanishing in the light. Glen crept over and scaled the short ladder beside her, the first faint smear of sunrise spreading below them.

"Pretty," he said.

She shrugged. "Don't tell that asshole you saw me here."

"Snakebite?"

"Roy."

Glen gripped the ladder hopefully. "You love Roy?"

33

She shook her head.

"So you're with him because he . . . buys you things?"

"What things? My little brother owes him money. Roy and I came up with this arrangement."

Glen felt a rush of horror and glee. Her affection suddenly seemed plausible. He hung there, trying to say the right thing. He wanted to explain why he hadn't stood up for the armadillo— because pissing Snakebite off might be dangerous—but that made him sound cowardly. Instead he said, "What would Roy do to your brother if you didn't honor your arrangement?"

Jalalieh glanced at him. "He's already done it."

"Done what?"

"He had that truck driver cut the toes off his foot with wire cutters."

Glen was about to change the subject, but she'd already swung to the tank below. By the time he descended, she was gone. He thought of the armadillo again, the knives, how Jalalieh had barreled in and taken control. It reminded him of the first time he'd accompanied his second ex-wife's father to a cockfight, which was illegal in Alabama. What had unsettled Glen wasn't the violence of the roosters pecking and spurring each other—he actually enjoyed betting on the bloody matches—but that several hippie-looking spectators had been smoking joints, right out in the open. Later he attributed his discomfort to that being his first and only experience outside the law.

Until now. Now the Black Beauty was a place with power up for grabs, a world where you fought for what you wanted, where you plotted, used force.

It was just getting light, time to shut down the plant, but Glen stood under the tanks, watching the dark office across the yard, where no doubt Roy slept like a king.

"Got-damn it, Glen," **Roy** said. "Ain't I told you to get some damn cable in here?"

Glen stood in his sneakers and baseball cap, Jalalieh behind him in the office door. "This is a business, not a residence," Glen said. "There's problems getting it installed."

"Then you better nigger-rig something by tomorrow night." Roy rose from his chair behind the desk, which had two portable TVs on it. "What?" he said to Jalalieh. "The little girl don't like that word? 'Nigger'?"

"Try 'African American,'" she said stiffly.

"Fuck that," he said. "I ain't no got-damn African American. I'm *American* American!"

She turned in a clatter of braids and vanished.

"And you," Roy said, "you got to clean this pigsty up."

Glen went cold. "Oh, Christ," he said. "When?"

"They flying in Wednesday night. Be here first thing Thursday."

Ernie and Dwight.

So in addition to his other work, Glen spent the night cleaning his plant. He patched holes and leaks with silicon. He welded, shoveled, sandblasted. Replaced filters and built new shaker screens and greased bone-dry fittings and paid Jalalieh fifty bucks to straighten the stockpiled material with the loader. By daybreak the place was in sterling shape and a solid black, grimy Glen trudged over to the office. He hid Roy's TVs in the closet. Sprayed Pledge and vacuumed the carpet and Windexed the windows and emptied an entire can of Lysol into the air. He flipped the calendar to—what month was it?—August.

No time to go home, so Glen showered in the break room,

using Snakebite's motel bar of Ivory soap and his sample-sized Head & Shoulders. When he stepped out, cinching his tie, it was seven, nearly time for the day shift to begin. He hurried to the plant to see things in the light. Perfect. Not a stray speck of grit. Gorgeous. In the office, he took out the ledgers and began to fudge. An hour later he looked up, his hand numb from erasing. Eight o'clock. They'd be here any second.

By ten they still hadn't arrived. The day-shifters had clocked in and, seeing the plant clean, understood there was an inspection and were working like they used to. For a moment, staring out the window at the humming plant and the legitimately loading trucks and the men doing constructive things in their safety equipment, Glen felt nostalgic and sad. He grabbed the phone.

"I said don't be calling this early," Roy growled.

"Where the hell are they?"

"Chill, baby. I had 'em met at the airport."

Images of Ernie and Dwight fingerless, mangled, swam before Glen's eyes. "My God." He sat down.

"Naw, baby." Roy chuckled. "I told a couple of my bitches to meet 'em. Them two old white mens ain't been treated this good they whole life."

"Hookers?" Glen switched ears. "So Ernie and Dwight aren't coming?"

"I expect they'll drop by for a few minutes," Roy said. "But Glen, if I was you, I wouldn't sweat E and D. If I was you, baby, I'd be scared of old Roy. I'd be coming up with some got-damn money and I'd be doing it fast."

True to Roy's word, Ernie and Dwight showed up in the afternoon, unshaven, red-eyed, smelling of gin and smiling, their ties loose, wedding rings missing. They stayed at the plant for half an hour, complimenting Glen on his appearance and on how spic-and-span his operation was. Keep up the good work, they said, falling back into their Caddy, and standing in the parking lot as they drove away, Glen saw a pink garter hanging from the rearview mirror.

Glen spent the rest of the day and most of his checking account bribing one of his ex-wives' old boyfriends, a cable installer, to run a line to the office. Then he went to apply for a home-improvement loan. Sitting across from the banker, who looked ten years younger, Glen stopped listening as soon as the guy said, "*Four* alimonies?"

Back at the plant, he hoped the new cable (including HBO and Cinemax) would ease Roy's temper. He filled the hopper and fired the plant up early. From behind the crusher he saw Roy drive up, saw him and Jalalieh get out. They didn't speak: Roy went into the office, carrying another TV, and Jalalieh stalked across the yard to the loader. She climbed in and started the engine, raced it to build air pressure. She goosed the levers, wiggling the bucket the way some people jingle keys. Catching Glen's eye, she drew a finger across her throat.

Just after dusk Snakebite's Peterbilt rumbled into the yard. It paused on the scales, then pulled next to the plant and stopped beneath the loading chute. Glen had the grit flowing before Snakebite's boots touched the ground. He stuffed his trembling hands into his pockets as the trucker shambled toward him.

"I'm real sorry, Slick," Snakebite mumbled, his eyes down. "It's nothing personal. Have you got the money? Any of it?"

Glen shook his head in disbelief, which also answered the question.

"I'll give you a few minutes," Snakebite said, "if you wanna get drunk. That helps a little."

Glen glanced at the dark office window—Roy would be there, watching.

"It won't be too bad," Snakebite said. "Roy needs you. He only wants me to take one of your little fingers, at the first knuckle. You even get to pick which one." He jerked a thumb behind him. "I keep some rubbing alcohol in the truck, and some Band-Aids. We can get you fixed up real quick. You better go on take you a swig, though." Snakebite had moved so close that Glen could smell Head & Shoulders shampoo.

He pointed toward the control room, and when Snakebite looked, Glen bolted for the ladder and shot up through the roaring darkness.

It was breezy at the top, warm fumes in the air from nearby insecticide plants. Backing away from the edge, Glen slipped and fell to one knee. He felt warm blood running down his bare leg. *"Jalalieh?"* he whispered. *"You up here?"* Searching for a weapon, he found the measuring tape with the bolt on the end. He scrambled to his feet and watched the side of the tank as it lit and faded, lit and faded.

In one flash of light a hand appeared, then another, then Snakebite's tiny head. His wide shoulders surfaced next, rubbing the ladder cage. On the tank, he wobbled uncertainly in his boots. He looked behind him, a hundred feet down, where his truck purred, still loading.

Glen let out a few feet of the measuring tape. Began swinging the bolt over his head like a mace.

"Slick!" Snakebite called. "Let's just get it over with. It won't even hurt till a few seconds after I do it. Just keep your hand elevated above your heart, and that'll help the throbbing."

He took a tentative step as a gust of hot, acrid wind swirled. He bent to roll up his pants leg, then disappeared as the light faded. When he appeared again, he held the Mississippi Gambler. "It's real sharp, Slick. Ain't no sawing involved. Just a quick cut and it's all over."

Glen moved back, swinging his mace, the shaker rattling beside him, the tank humming beneath his sneakers. He stepped onto the metal gridwork of a catwalk and the ground appeared for a moment, far below, then vanished. When the light came again Snakebite loomed in front of him. Glen yelled and the mace flew wildly to the right.

Snakebite struck him in the chest with a giant forearm that sent Glen skidding across the catwalk, his cap fluttering away. He tried to rise, but the truck driver pinned him flat on his belly, his right arm twisted behind him.

"Hold your breath, Slick," Snakebite grunted.

Glen fisted his left hand and felt hot grit. With his teeth clenched, he slung it over his shoulder.

Snakebite yelled, let him go. Glen rolled and saw the big man staggering backward, clawing at his eyes.

There was only the one ladder down, and Snakebite had it blocked, so Glen began to circle the shaker. A glint of something white bounced off the rail by his hand—the Mississippi Gambler—and Snakebite charged, the trench knife gleaming.

Glen dodged and, running for the ladder, got pegged in the shoulder by the shaker. He spun, grabbing his arm, and fell, kicking at Snakebite, who swiped halfheartedly with the trench knife. Glen scrabbled to his feet and feinted, but the truck driver moved with him, and Glen was cornered. Snakebite, pulsing in and out of the darkness, lifted his giant hand as if someone had just introduced them.

Glen slowly raised his right hand, balled in a fist. "How could you cut off her brother's toes?" he yelled.

"Whose brother?" Snakebite grabbed Glen's hand and forced the pinky out. "Don't watch," he said.

Glen closed his eyes, expecting the cut to be ice-cold at first. But the howl in the air was not, he thought, coming from him. He opened one eye and put his fist (pinky intact) down. The truck driver, clutching his tiny head with both hands, still had the trench knife hooked to his fingers. Behind him, Jalalieh was backing away with an iron pipe in her fist. Snakebite dropped the trench knife and fell to his knees. He rolled on his side and curled into a ball.

Glen picked up the knife.

"Come on," Jalalieh hissed. "Roy's on his way!"

They hurried across the tanks and the spotlights flared, as if the Black Beauty were about to lift off into the night. Glen knew Roy had flipped the master breaker below. Jalalieh took his arm and they crept to the rail. Roy was pulling himself up, sweaty, scowling, a snub-nosed pistol in one hand. Glen began to kick grit off the edge to slow him.

"Got-damn it!" Roy yelled, and a bullet sang straight up into the night, a foot from Glen's chin.

"Jesus!" He pushed Jalalieh behind him and they stumbled back. Glen remembered a proposal he'd sent Ernie and Dwight a year ago—one that called for another access way to the top, stairs or a caged elevator.

A long minute passed before Roy finally hoisted himself onto the tanks, grit glittering on his cheeks and forehead. Breathing hard, he transferred the pistol to the hand holding the rail and with the other removed his fedora and dusted himself off. He took a cigar from his shirt pocket and chomped on it but didn't try lighting it.

"Girl," he said to Jalalieh. "Get over here."

She left Glen, careful of the shaker, more careful of Roy.

"Get your ass down there and fill up that got-damn hopper," he ordered. "It's fixing to run out."

She shot Glen a look he couldn't identify, then disappeared down the ladder.

"Snakebite!" Roy yelled.

The big driver stirred, grit pouring off him. He rubbed the back of his head with one hand and his eyes with the other. There was blood on his collar and fingers. He blinked at Roy.

"Shit, baby," Roy laughed, "we wear hard hats in the plant for a reason, right, Glen?"

Snakebite, his eyes lowered, limped across the catwalk and stuffed himself into the ladder cage.

Holding the pistol loosely at his side, Roy watched Glen. "You want something done right," he muttered, "don't send no stupid-ass Texas redneck." He slipped the gun into his pants pocket and turned, walked toward the ladder. "I'm gonna garnish your salary," he called over his shoulder, "till your debt's paid off."

Glen followed him, his heart rattling in his chest. When he lifted his hand to cover his eyes, he saw the trench knife.

Roy was crossing the catwalk, holding the rails on either side, when Glen lunged and hit him in the back of the neck with the brass knuckles. The cigar shot from his mouth and Roy was surprisingly easy—a hand on his belt, one on his collar—to offset and shove over the rail. Falling, Roy opened his mouth but no sound came out. With eyes that looked incredibly hurt, he dropped, arms wheeling, legs running. He was screaming now, shrinking, turning an awkward somersault. Glen looked away before he hit the concrete.

,　　,　　,

On the ground, Glen could feel the tanks vibrating in his legs. He took deep breaths, hugging himself, and felt better. His heart was still there, hanging on, antique maybe, shot full of holes and eroded nearly to nothing, but still, by God, pumping. He went to a line of breakers and flipped one. The spotlights died.

He heard footsteps, and Jalalieh ran past him in the dark. Glen reached for her but she was gone. He followed. They found Snakebite standing by Roy's body. He'd thrown a tarp over him.

"He slipped," Glen said.

"Right." Jalalieh ran her brown eyes over Glen, then looked up into the darkness. "He must've."

"God almighty," Snakebite said. He rubbed his nose. For a moment Glen thought the truck driver was crying, but it was just grit in his eyes.

Jalalieh knelt and pulled back the tarp. There was blood. Without flinching, she went through Roy's pockets and found his gun, the keys to his car, his roll of money and his ledger. She stood, and Glen and Snakebite followed her into the control room. Inside, she studied the ledger. Looking over her shoulder, Glen saw an almost illegible list that must have been Roy's grit clients. He strained to read them but Jalalieh flipped to a list of names and numbers. Glen's own debt, he noticed, was tiny in comparison to Snakebite's, and to Jalalieh's.

Jalalieh's?

Glen frowned. "What about your little brother?"

"What brother?" She licked her thumb and began counting the money. Behind her, Snakebite sat heavily in a chair.

"So, wait," Glen said, "you were paying Roy by, by—"

"By fucking, Glen." She glanced at him. "You want it spelled out, little man? He was fucking you one way and me another way. And the truth is, you were getting the better deal."

"What now?" Snakebite asked, his voice like gravel.

"You deliver, same as always," Jalalieh said. "And keep quiet. Nothing's changed."

With the truck driver gone, Glen grew suddenly nauseated. He crossed the room and took a hard hat from the rack and filled it with a colorless liquid. He closed his eyes and breathed through his nose.

At the control panel, Jalalieh tapped the dryer's temperature gauge. "How hot does this thing get?"

Glen had cold sweats. "Thousand degrees Fahrenheit," he said, which didn't seem nearly enough to warm him.

She smiled. "Shut the plant down."

Half an hour later things were very quiet, only the fiddling of crickets from nearby trees. Jalalieh came in the loader. Glen looked away while she scooped Roy, tarp and all, off the ground.

He walked through the plant, pausing to kick open a cutoff valve that released a hissing cloud of steam. At the dryer, Jalalieh lowered the bucket and dumped Roy's body. One of his shoes had come off. In heavy gloves, Glen turned the wheel that opened the furnace door. It took them both to lift the fat man and, squinting against the heat, to cram him into the chamber. Jalalieh pitched his fedora in, then sent Glen after the shoe. By the time they'd closed the door and locked the wheel, they could see through the thick yellowed porthole that Roy's clothes and hair had caught fire.

Jalalieh followed Glen into the control room and watched him press buttons and adjust dials, the plant puffing and groaning as it stirred to life. She said she wanted to ignite the dryer, and when it came time to set the temperature she cranked the knob into the red. For an hour they sat quietly, passing Glen's flask back and forth, while Roy burned in the dryer, while his charred bones were pounded to dust in the crusher and dumped into the shaker, which clattered madly, sifting the remains of Roy Jones through the screens and sending him through various chutes and depositing the tiny flecks, according to size, into the storage tanks.

Two weeks later Jalalieh called the plant, collect. She told Glen that Ernie and Dwight were slated for another surprise inspection on September fifth. She gave him the phone numbers of two reliable hookers. Then she read him her account number in the bank where Glen was to deposit her cut. She wouldn't give her location, but said she lived alone, in a cabin, and there was snow. That she jogged every day up mountains, through tall trees. That she'd taken a part-time job at a logging plant, for the fun of it, driving a front-end loader. "Only here they call it a skidder," she told him.

"Ja—" he said, but she'd hung up.

He replaced the phone and leaned back in his chair. Propped his feet on his desk. It was time to throw himself head, body and heart into work. He speed-dialed Snakebite on the cellular phone and told him to be at the plant by eight. Tonight would be busy. You'd think, from all the sandblasting grit they were selling, that the entire hull of the world was caked and corroded with rust, barnacles and scum, and that somebody, somewhere, was finally cleaning things up.

For Uncle D, Robert, Steve, Jim, Simon and Bryan

shubuta

Welcome to Shubuta.

Look around. Abandoned tractors eaten up with kudzu. Flat land, high distorted sun, dry fields. Along the road in a dirt yard walleyed children hunch over a circle of dusty marbles, still as a picture. A black lady carrying an empty laundry basket walks against traffic. There are shiny cars and houses on blocks. I lift another can from the ice and pop the tab and let the beer run down my throat.

This is what I think: Dying in a hospital can go to hell. You've got to cash in violently, with some honor—rescue a baby from railroad tracks, get done in yourself by the train. Smother a hand grenade in combat and save eleven buddies, something like that. The pistol to the head's an option, but you need a creative twist.

Take Willie Howe. He was a black watermelon farmer who lived right here in Shubuta, Mississippi. He stood thirty ripe melons along his fence and duct-taped reading glasses to each one and shot them through the left lenses. Then he went in the house, crawled under the bed and shot himself in the right lens. The newspaper said his brother-in-law was a white optometrist in Mobile. His name's Ted. When I went to see him, Ted told me Willie's suicide was the best advertisement he'd ever had. Looking into my eyes with a penlight, Ted told me Willie did it because his old lady left him.

"Love goes bad all over," Ted said.

,   ,   ,

I've been spending nights driving by my ex-girlfriend's with my lights off. Her name's Diane; we both live over near Mobile. When she didn't come back to her house last night, I went to price pistols at Wal-Mart, but instead had my biorhythms read by a machine in the mall. It cost a quarter, and you put your finger in this little hole. My creativity reading was off the scale on the high side. Sex and romance were way, way down. Health, drive, endurance, finance, friendship and luck were medium to low. I photocopied the printout at a gas station and slipped it under her door.

I thought about my uncle Dock, who's dying. How love went bad for him after he'd been married only two months. This was in the 1940s, and now, fifty years later, he won't talk about it unless he's drunk. If you mention his marriage when he's sober, he changes the subject. He'll tell you about his younger sister, Nannie-Rae. "Oh, she had herself a way with birds," he'll say. "She could whistle any birdsong there was, and goddamn jaybirds used to perch on her finger and circle around her head. Damnedest thing. Even chickens'd follow her."

Or he might tell about his daddy's—my granddaddy's—drinking. How the old man was drunk one afternoon and forgot to pick up Dock and Nannie-Rae from school. Dock was eight, Nannie-Rae six. Walking the dirt road home, they held hands and sang songs. It was three miles, dry weather. High up a hawk circled, and as the children walked, eyeing the bird, a log truck barreled around the curve, enclosing them in dust. Dock yelled and yanked Nannie-Rae out of the road, hurting her arm. She was crying, holding her shoulder, when she stepped defiantly back into the road.

The second log truck dragged her two hundred feet. Dock ran after, dropping his schoolbooks. He ran past her shoes, scraps of her dress. By the time he got to the truck the driver had his coat spread over her. It was a black man and he caught Dock and said, "Don't look, don't look."

Dock kicked till he was let go, and he ran tumbling into the woods. A group of Primitive Baptists found him after dark, wandering around. He didn't remember anything. They snapped their fingers in his face but he just stared. His mother was at the hospital, praying by the bed. Nannie-Rae was still alive, but the doctor told the mother her daughter wouldn't live much longer. The father was in his truck. He drove to the road where he found her shoes and he picked up the pieces of her dress and put them in his pocket. He lifted a pail from the truck and with a shovel dug the blood from the road, stopping only to drink from his bottle.

Uncle Dock will tell you all he remembers about Nannie-Rae now are the birds. He doesn't even know what she looked like. The truck driver began stuttering after the accident and couldn't stop talking about the little girl he'd killed. Until he died, he would visit Uncle Dock's parents once or twice a year, and when they died he visited Uncle Dock. He would be drunk, crying, and though it took him a long time, he retold the story exactly the same way. How the birds stopped singing. *You you you you eyes was dis dis dis big, Muh Muh Muh Muh Mister Dock . . .*

Diane cried, too, when I told her that story, though some of it was stuff I'd had to imagine. Then I told her more, how after Uncle Dock's wife left him in the 1940s, he fished summer evenings in the river behind the chemical plant where he worked. He ran trotlines, shot yawning cottonmouths out of trees from his skiff. Beer on the water, standing to aim a stream of piss at the smooth blue catfish. Throwing the ones he didn't want on the floor of the boat—grinnel, carp, suckers: trash fish, bottom feeders. *Give 'em to the niggers,* he'd say, *they eat anything.*

Hunting in the fall. Cool weather, steamy breath, moving like a ghost through woods. Uncle Dock calling up gobblers, yepping, their wily approach, bobbing heads, eyes like marble: *Come a little closer, Mr. Turkey, that's it, yep yep yep, move into range, that's it, and, and . . . ah!*

Drinking out of jars, a thousand gallons of homemade whisky. Lighting a million Camel cigarettes. Raising from pups a dozen fine coon dogs, one or two at a time, until they died, ran off or got killed: Herbert and Hoover, Sidney, Dan'l Boone, January, Abraham, Decent, Chickenshit, Otis, Rotten, Coon Ass and Jesus H. Christ. They slept outside, on the porch in a wooden box with a blanket in winter and under the house by the kitchen pipes in summer. He would shoot stray cats on sight and pay black boys a nickel to tote off the carcasses.

For forty-two years Uncle Dock worked at the chemical plant, making DDT, until it was banned by the EPA, then making diazinon until last year's retirement party, a gold plaque, and we got drunk on his porch.

Fresh out of the army, I was staying with him. The whisky tasted like gasoline and ate the bottoms out of Styrofoam cups, and I got the feeling he knew I was lying about my rank of corporal. He had served, too. The draft. Flying home after fighting for his country to a woman who would leave him.

"Uncle Dock," I said, "tell me the truth about your marriage."

"Lasted ever bit of two months," he told me, pouring us more whisky.

"What happened?"

"They was somebody else."

"Another man?"

"Yep."

"What'd you do?"

"Nothing." He poured himself more whisky. "The hell could I do, boy?"

"Fight for her," I said. "Kill the son of a bitch."

"Lord, I thought about it many an evening," he said, raising his glass.

Last night I rode the elevator with Jack Daniel's in my pocket. Hospital halls, long and white. Gray wainscotting for my fingers to run along. Belching. I got lost and asked and somebody showed me his room. I'd been standing right beside it. I tapped on the door and went in. He looked skinnier and was a paler color, but he just started talking like we were on his porch and nothing was wrong.

"They's this big fat lady moved in that old place beside me back at the house," he said. "Real porker. She wears this sombrero-looking gardening hat and these koo-lots and the cheeks of her ass hang out like I couldn't tell you. I watch her through the whaddyacallit, the blinds. From my bedroom window. This fellow, a hippie, comes sees her once or twice a week and they set out on her back porch, giggling. He's skinny as a damn rail. Shit, I get to giggling with 'em myself some days. The lady, she brings out beer and they toast after everything they say, and pretty soon they look around real shrewd-like to see if anybody's watching, though there ain't nobody on that whole damn street except for me, and I'm in there in the dark, dead for all they know. So she brings out this plastic bag of reefer and he gets his papers and they roll a big fat one and fire up.

"Thing is, I can't figure out if it's the hippie bringing her the weed or if she grows it herself in that backyard jungle of hers. Sometimes he'll get up and go wading through the weeds and fall down and plumb disappear. She spits out beer she's laughing so hard. Then he stands up and they go inside holding hands. Shut the door and crawl all over each other, I reckon."

I got out of my chair.

Morphine pumped into his arm, a thin white tube.

"Your momma tells me you done fell in love," he said, closing his eyes.

I was looking out the window. Dark: car lights five floors down.

"Her name's Diane," I said. "We broke up."

In the bathroom later while Uncle Dock slept, I snapped the tab of a diet Coke and poured half of it down the sink and re-placed it with whisky. I heard sudden sharp dry coughs and hurried to his side and touched his arm. Dribble ran down his chin, his eyes rolled back. *Hunh,* he went, leaning up, *hunh hunh.* I could feel the coughs rattling in my own rib cage. Then a tall black nurse brushed me aside saying I'd have to leave, my time was up.

Shubuta. Population 614.

Light-headed, sweating beer. Kudzu. Crows standing stiff-legged around a distant dead thing. Fields on both sides: corn, dying.

Thinking of Willie Howe's suicide, I pull off the road next to a rust-bucket pickup truck full of watermelons. This old black dude sits there asleep in a ragged easy chair under a big purple umbrella with his head on his fist and his loafers propped on his tailgate. There's a hand-lettered sign on the truck that says WATERMELONS 3/$5.

After I've stolen like nine melons I get worried the old dude might be dead. So I ease the van door shut and go over and poke his shoulder.

"Hey," I say. "Wake up, pops."

His eyes open.

"You know Willie Howe?" I ask him. "The fellow shot all those watermelons?"

He straightens in the chair, shows pink gums but no teeth when he opens his mouth to cough. Then he says, "You gonna buy some melons?"

"Could be. I bet these're right out of Willie's fields, right?"

"You buying?"

"Some mighty fine specimens you got here," I tell him.

"Thumpable ripe," he says. "My wife, she a voodoo doctor and she know just when to pick 'em. She say, 'Cleavon, this one ripe and this here one ripe, but that'n over yonder need to set three more days.' You want some?"

"How much?"

"Can't you read?"

"Well."

"It's right on that sign there, and I don't like nobody axing they price when there it go in plain sight."

"Your wife a voodoo doctor?"

"I just said that. Don't like nobody axing me is she a voodoo doctor when I just said it."

"Can she fix me a potion so my girlfriend'll come back?"

"You damn right."

"She can do that I don't need any watermelons."

An eighteen-wheeler carrying cattle roars by, a stink of manure and diesel.

He looks at me from the watery bottoms of his eyes. "When my old lady want a melon to eat, she tell me throw her some off on the ground. She mean hard, so they bust open. Juice flying everywhere. Then she make me fetch the heart out each one of them melons on the ground all split up, put that cool red heart in a bowl, give it to her. She eat it all. But only that heart. Rest just rurn." He moves his feet from the tailgate and plants them on the ground and gazes at the melons. "You know how long it take to grow a good-size melon like these here?"

"No, sir."

"Take a long time. I sell these babies, make a fine profit, 'less I know you. I know you, I cut you a deal. But I don't know you, now, do I?"

I don't say anything and he looks into the curves and humps of the melons in his truck.

"Lemme ax you a question," he says. "How come I throw them perfectly good melons and bust 'em open just so she can gobble that heart out?"

"You got me."

"This girlfriend, she ever make you poke chops?"

"Oh, man."

"Son, you pitiful! Don't never eat no meat a woman give you. They carry it in they panties and administrate on it before they cook it, and you eat it you theirs for life. That how my old lady caught me. You'll do anything they say once they put the hex on you. You can't get away."

"Well, it don't sound so bad, if it's the right woman."

"Ain't no such thing! Bible say the man supposed to rule the house. You don't want your girlfriend voodoo smoking up your judgment."

"She don't know about voodoo. All she can do is look good."

"Voodoo voodoo."

What if that's what happened to old Willie Howe, I think. Did some witch-woman get hold of him voodoo-wise? Did it break his heart to toss his hard work in the dirt for her? I picture Willie making his escape. He leaves her sleeping, her afternoon nap, a hot breeze coming through the rusty screens. He takes from the nightstand the snub-nosed thirty-eight, slips it and two boxes of cartridges into his pockets. He goes out through the tall summer weeds with grasshoppers springing up. In his pickup he drives to the most remote corner of his farm, the box of eyeglasses on the seat beside him.

"Poor old Willie," I say.

"Poor old us all," the watermelon man says.

In the van, its rear end weighted down with melons, I dig in the cooler and find a beer. The landscape passes, two skinny silhouettes fighting with sling blades. My clothes and hair are damp from sweat, the four o'clock sun in my eyes. I come to a rest area and rumble off the road. Not a fancy place like on the interstate, this one just pine trees and a few rotten picnic tables, a garbage can. Kudzu climbs the trees, scales power poles, goes wire to wire.

My cigarette package, empty, flutters to the ground. A far-off buzzard doing wide, slow turns above the tree line is the only thing moving. Uncle Dock calls them country airplanes, the way they glide. He says your average buzzard can see for miles. I suppose that old fellow up there can see me clear as day, though he's just a speck from here.

If he's looking now, he sees me close my eyes. I'm imagining a young, healthy Uncle Dock going after the man who stole his wife. I make the thief a curly-headed half-breed from Shubuta, a high yellow giant with a hearty laugh. He is handy with knives. I pour straight rotgut down Uncle Dock for three days, bring him red-eyed and reckless to Shubuta with nothing to lose. My family knows how to work a shotgun. How to drink. Uncle Dock, reeling, pictures thick fingers undoing his wife's dress and a bone-hard torso pressing her against a door, a big red tongue in her ear as the half-breed seizes her by her wet crotch with one hand and lifts her off the floor. Her high heel shoes fall off: *thump,* the left one, *thump,* the right.

Hearing her cries, Uncle Dock stops in the hall. Clutches his face. Turns the shotgun.

I open the van's back door from the inside.

An old yellow dog with gnats around his ears regards me from one of the picnic tables. His tongue hangs out, and he doesn't even blink when I approach, cradling a watermelon. I flick open my pocketknife and cut into the rind. The dog's ears twitch, his drab tail wags. I reach over and shake the scruff of his neck.

"Half for you, half for me," I say.

Without rising he sticks his head down in the bowl of melon and laps.

I think of Diane. Her sweet salty pussy. When I called her on the phone last week she said, "Somebody who goes on and on about suicide used to be considered not likely to carry out."

I said, "What do you mean used to be?"

She said, "Now psychology's changed and you're actually dangerous."

Dangerous. It gave me a spiny thrill, being dangerous.

poachers

, . .

The evening air, crowded with bats and the bugs the bats eat. At Uncle Dock's house, while the dog gnaws chicken bones from the floor next to the refrigerator, the room grows dark around us. I sit with my elbows on the table and light a cigarette. Blow a thin jet of smoke toward the window. Watch cloudy shapes rise and swirl in the Mason jar before me. The love potion. It looks like plain river water, infested with bacteria and sludge from chemical plants. Sewage. I unscrew the lid and there's a muddy grating, the dog growling softly over his bones.

When I finish my cigarette, I'll go into the bedroom and sit in Uncle Dock's chair and press my forehead against the windowpane and spy next door: they'll be sitting there smoking pot, fat lady and hippie, in love. They'll toast and toke and giggle, and I'll giggle too, and so will Uncle Dock when I sneak into the intensive care unit later and tell him how, after getting sky-high, they stumbled into her house and the lights snapped on, how I slipped outside and climbed the fence between the properties and crept through the high weeds of her yard. How I placed my eye against the window and saw they'd taken the missionary position, Patsy Cline crackling on the turntable. How a dusty gray moth flaring in my eyes causes me to tumble backwards into the reefer plants, how I just lie there with my eyes closed and the earth spinning, and the lovers come to the window with a bedsheet covering their bodies, and they frown and whisper, but instead of the fat lady I imagine it's Diane I see, and my heart lurches murderously, but I don't move and they don't notice me lying there, among the weeds, in the darkness.

triathlon

The bachelor party started Friday night: a dozen horny drunks careening among the strip bars and the neon smoke. We left guys asleep in their cars and passed out at tables and propped in alleys, until Bruce and I were the only ones left. Just after dawn he hot-wired a Jeep we found in a parking lot and there were all these expensive rods and reels in the back. So we headed over the bridge to Dauphin Island, half an hour's drive from Mobile, for the shark fishing.

Prissy's was a tiny dive on the west side of the island, the last stop before the oyster-shell road ended and you needed a four-wheel-drive to go farther. Inviting beer signs gleamed in the windows. The pool games cost seventy-five cents each and we knew Paul, the bartender. He used to work at the chemical plant with us. We were night watchmen. Prissy was his old lady and she owned the bar, but she was divorcing him, and until she fired him and kicked him out, he'd give his friends drinks on the house.

The parking lot was empty and Paul was alone, playing the blackjack machine, when we walked in. Bruce went to get quarters for the pool table.

"Man, where is everybody?" he asked.

I went through the swinging doors to the pay phone and punched up Jan's number.

"It's six A.M.," she said. "Where in the world are you?"

I told her.

"*Jesus.*"

"Look—" I said.

But she'd hung up.

When I stepped out Bruce and Paul were playing eight ball. I walked to the pool table.

Bruce glanced at me. "Everything hunky-dory?"

"Swell."

Paul handed me a beer. "Bruce says you're getting married, you idiot."

I looked at my watch. "Tonight."

"Shit. Why?"

Bruce looked up from the table. "Because the rabbit died."

Paul lit a cigarette and smoked. His eyes were red. Balls clacked on the felt and thumped as they died in their pockets. Bruce moved around the table, smoking and inspecting the layout of things.

"Nine, side," he said, and then it was.

Paul drained his cup, then went over behind the bar.

I watched Bruce puzzling at the table, chalking his cue. He shook another cigarette from his pack and lit it and sipped his beer. He was older than I was, and taller. He was an ex-marine, had survived a tour of duty in Vietnam. He'd come home and witnessed the Kent State massacre in 1970. He'd played semipro baseball in Italy after that, been an extra in a spaghetti Western, done acid on a subway in Japan.

But this was all before I knew him.

What we did together was run—he bragged that he'd come in 314th in the '83 Chicago Marathon—and drink. We met at work and started going to bars together. We'd run in local marathons on weekends, get drunk afterward.

In a few minutes Paul brought over a pitcher of margaritas, a thick crust of salt on the rim. He poured me one and I tasted it. "I've been here for four days without going home," he said.

"Your shot," Bruce told him.

Paul nodded sadly. He walked over and, trying to make the four, knocked in the eight ball. We moved and stood on either side of him and Bruce asked him to come fishing with us. Paul said he had to stay, in case the phone rang. Bruce said he was crazy, told him to shut his eyes, for God's sake. To picture us there on the edge of the island, fishing until the sun went down and the moon rose from the bay, our lines stretched out of sight and heavy with cut bait, the three of us propped in aluminum chairs and drinking cold beer from one of Prissy's kegs, our rods leaping in our hands as the sand sharks hit, and then the long, exhausting battle of pulling them in. We'd build a giant bonfire out of driftwood, the shark spines lighting up on the sand, the rubbery blue skin turned inside out, the black dead eyes. We'd have to keep sliding our chairs back as the tide closed in and— near dawn—took the fire, an early fog drifting out over the water, the long, mournful foghorns sounding from shrimp boats trolling the bay.

I grew anxious to get there, just listening, but Paul wouldn't go. He stood wobbling in the door of his wife's empty bar holding her half-empty pitcher, and as we drove away I watched him until he dissolved and I turned, saw that we were headed west, away from the wedding that was gathering behind us.

When the baby is born dead, there's no reason to stay married. I'm on day shift at the plant. At night I drink zombies at Judge

Roy Bean's until I think Jan's ready for bed and I come home and try to fool around. She says no, or doesn't say anything, just waits until I realize she isn't going to answer, and I slam the door and go into the den and fall asleep on the sofa with the TV on.

One night, when I come in, she tells me she's still spotting.

I ask her what she wants to do.

"I want to cry," she says.

Judge's is always full of laughing flirting women who'll let you buy them drinks. I'm on speaking terms with the bartender, and when I go back in that night he says, "Here's the man with the plan!" and I say, "Where, where?" looking cleverly behind me, and he laughs and starts my tab.

In the morning, the phone next to the sofa rings. I sit up. It's Bruce—he's been gone for seven months, since the wedding.

He says, "How's married life?"

"What day is it?"

"Saturday?"

Jan stands in the bedroom doorway in her white gown. She's pale, thin, the dark under her eyes like mascara that's run from crying.

When I hang up, she says, "Who was that?"

I don't say anything, but she knows.

"That asshole," she says. "Is he coming here?"

"We'll go out."

She hugs herself. "It's not supposed to be like this."

Bruce arrives on a Triumph. I throw a leg over and he revs the motor and we're off, Jan watching from the kitchen window, holding herself. Bruce pulls a flask from his pocket and hands it over his shoulder. I drink dizzily and feel the wind lift the hair from my scalp. On the Bayway Bridge we use the hazard lanes to pass cars, swerve to miss something dead. You can see over the rails to the water below; you could let your fingers drag along the concrete.

We sling through the Bankhead Tunnel and fly through the blinking downtown caution lights, then hit the interstate and ride two nonstop hours to Evergreen, where Bruce leans the bike onto an off-ramp and we roll into a Texaco station. "Got your plastic?" he asks, and I tap my wallet. He pumps the gas, I pay and load the supplies—beef jerky, two six-packs, M&Ms, cigarettes—into the bike's knapsack. I go around the side of the building and take the pay phone from its cradle and try to think of what to say to Jan.

There isn't anything.

So Bruce and I peel off, leaving a long thin black strip of tire on the road behind us—probably the only evidence Bruce leaves anywhere. But there's evidence of me everywhere, on the credit-card receipt in the gas station's register, a time card at the chemical plant, a bleeding woman in my house, a child's white marble tombstone.

Back on the interstate I close my eyes and see Jan putting things into a suitcase. She isn't crying but she looks hollow and sick. She slips her wedding band off and sets it on the nightstand. Then keeps packing.

I remember the last time I saw Bruce, the shark fishing, riding on the beach, half in, half out of the surf. Having to roll up the window to keep the waves from crashing in. Bruce driving the way he drives, better drunk than sober, things appearing before us, malevolent driftwood shapes, sudden boulders, a sofa. Not catching a shark, not even a nibble.

Passing out on the tip of the island, waking up sunburned.

poachers

Not remembering how I got home, somebody feeding me coffee an hour before the wedding.

Jan saying, "How could you?"

Maybe I was in the kitchen, maybe throwing up in the sink.

Her bridesmaids there, whispering.

Bruce missing the wedding. No best man.

How back from the long, silent honeymoon, I called Paul at
Prissy's and he said Bruce had quit his job at the plant and set
out for New York.

Jan saying, "Good riddance." My ridiculous sunburned face
in the wedding pictures.

Paul trying to set Prissy's afire and being arrested.

After a couple more hours on the bike, Bruce and I stop under
a bridge for a smoke. He says it was too cold in New York; he'd
ridden back, decided it was time to get quote responsible. He says
he found a job as a hose man in a chicken-processing plant. They
killed a hundred and fifty thousand broilers a day. Millions of
gallons of blood, Bruce says. It ran into the sewer like a river.
That was in Guntersville, Alabama. He stayed there for two
weeks, ten working days, a million and a half dead birds.

He met a woman named Patty there. He left her there.

"She was a health nut, a vegetarian," Bruce says. "Into hiking
and shit. But she showed me this one place that I'm fixing to
show you."

We get back on the bike and ride for another hour. Green
signs naming places come and go and I doze until he slows the
bike. An exit says Guntersville. We pull off the interstate, cut
right at a two-lane and Bruce walks the bike up to seventy. We're
leaving civilization, I decide. An hour later he slows and takes a
dirt road for a mile, two, the cornfields swelling to trees and the

trees closing in. Past a no-trespassing sign, Bruce turns onto a path I wouldn't have seen. Vines hang and we creep along, ducking low limbs, parting the leaves with our fingers.

In a clearing we dismount.

"As far as el bike-o can go," he explains.

"Where the hell are we?"

He grins and tosses me the knapsack, tells me there's shorts inside. He peels down to his running shorts and stuffs his boots and clothes into the knapsack, puts on his running shoes and takes off.

I haven't run much since being married so I expect my legs to cramp, but they feel great, never stronger, drumming over the soft carpet of leaves, hurtling stumps and tiny creek beds.

We've covered about a mile when Bruce darts right, into a damp pine grove. I follow blindly, not thinking. Another mile passes, the undergrowth webbing, the treetops closing like fingers making a steeple. Behind Bruce I duck and dodge the sudden obstacles he creates, the whip of a limb, angry flurries from a hornets' nest tipped by his elbow. He stumbles, goes faster. Then, half a mile farther, as we're more falling than running, fingers dragging along the earth, the trees on both sides of us fly apart, as if painted on curtains.

Unable to stop, I crash into him and nearly shove him into the sky—the sky mirrored in water, a lake, still as perfect glass, large as a baseball diamond, there at our feet.

Bruce steps back and kicks off his shoes. He dives into the water and doesn't emerge until he's ten yards out, his arms breaking the surface, pulling him toward the white limestone bank across the lake.

I follow him in, the water so deep I go under, so cold I come up gasping. I yell, begin to swim, following his distant explosions.

I get a quick taste of fear on my lips but the water between my toes and fingers holds me high, and in minutes I'm swimming alongside Bruce. He nods at the bank.

The bank, ten million years of limestone layers compacted against one another, is tall and hollowed, a bowl upside down, a cave whose rim rises five feet out of the water and spans forty feet. We move toward it, our strokes slowing as we near its mouth. We draw ourselves close enough to the cave to see the strange film of green algae that clings to the sunlit interior walls. Higher on the walls, where the sun doesn't reach, there's only rock. In a courageous spell, I move to go inside, to follow the dark, wide tunnel whose end you can't see, but Bruce grabs my shoulder and leads me away from the bank. We tread water with our arms and legs, and wait. Behind us the sun disappears beyond the treetops, darkness rolling as oil might across the lake's surface toward our heads that stick out of the water like rocks. I stretch my toes down, find nothing except deeper water, and suddenly I grow frightened, bobbing uselessly here in the middle of a lake, in the middle of the woods, in the middle of nowhere.

"They're coming," Bruce says.

There will be a time.

It will be after Jan has left and come back, left and come back. It may be years from now.

I'll be living in a shithole apartment and working graveyards at the chemical plant again and drinking too much. Some nights deserting my post and jogging the plant's perimeter, avoiding the security patrols and cameras, taking to the woods, scaring up deer and setting off quail.

Bruce will come back.

He'll be waiting on my steps early one morning as I'm getting home from work. He'll crack jokes about punching a time clock. He'll tell me he sold the Triumph in Tempe, Arizona, and moved in with a Navajo woman for too many months, then stole her Trans Am and drove to California to live with his friend Laura, an actress. That he got a bit part in a Robert De Niro gangster film and somebody recognized him and the FBI found him and he did time. That when he was released after two years, he rode the bus east across the country. He watched the states pass him by, buttes and deserts and oil wells and famous rivers and markers of historical events. Outside El Paso they passed a huddle of Mexicans standing in their yard watching their house burn down. In another bus he crossed Louisiana during the dark early morning hours with a plastic flask in his pocket, watching his cigarette tip glow in the window, reading the names of places and trying to remember if he knew anybody from there.

His ticket took him as far as Jackson, Mississippi, and he hitched the rest of the way back.

We'll sit in front of the TV and pop the tabs of Bud Lights and I'll give him the lowdown at the plant, tell him he can maybe get his old job back. But he'll laugh and say, "No fucking way."

He'll say he's going to Alaska or someplace, to see the northern lights.

"What I need," he'll say, "is a ride."

I'll decide I can't see Jan that night. I'll call and cancel dinner, will listen to her voice on the phone for a long time, knowing she's telling the truth, but then somehow hang softly up.

Maybe Bruce and I will go by and steal her old Toyota and head out of town, drive north on back roads, through the country.

We'll notice things: three hawks in the same dead tree. A flatbed truck hauling a steeple. A child's wheelchair in front of a trailer. We'll drink beer and stop to piss along the road between the towns, Creola, Axis, Bucks, Sunflower, Mount Vernon, Calvert, McIntosh. Wagerville, Leroy, Jackson, Grove Hill. Fulton. Then, just north of Thomasville, heading for Selma, there'll be something big glinting at us through the trees at the top of a hill. An old fire tower, abandoned, a metal skeleton covered with kudzu.

I'll leave the road and nose the car into the woods, forget to close my door as I get out and race Bruce up the hill to the tower. Against the sky, the tree trunks are a deep somber gray. Bruce will stand under the tower pissing again and looking up where the sky is rushing past the cabin. A few early dim stars move in and out of the clouds. I imagine a park ranger climbing the tower with a pair of binoculars and a thermos of coffee, maybe a book, spending his hours looking across the distance, seeing for miles, dreading and hoping to spot a dark arm of smoke reaching up out of the woods. The CLIMB AT YOUR OWN RISK sign is faded and overrun with kudzu, which shimmers on the tower like lace and has taken the hill like an army.

Still looking up, I step on something and turn my ankle, reach down into the kudzu. It's the front leg of a deer, sawed off below the knee: delicate, light brown fur, sharp black two-toed hoof, white tip of hair halfway up. It weighs nothing, like the batons that track teams pass. I roll it in my palm, feel the speed in my grip, hand it to Bruce. When we kick around in the kudzu we find dozens of the legs, front and back, scattered over the ground. Fanning out, we find the bleached skulls of deer, hides stiff as pieces of wood, antlers. We're standing in carnage. You can smell a trace of death in the air, it comes at you on the wind.

Bruce motions at the tower. "Poachers shoot 'em from up there."

I leave him examining one of the legs and start up the tower. The bottom flight of steps is missing, to discourage climbers, but I put my beer in my pocket and scale the girders, finding footholds on rivets and splayed lips of metal. The upper flights are intact and easy to climb, the trunks of pine trees thinning with altitude, and with a lightening in the pit of my stomach I climb past the treetops and the sky swells around me. Now I'm moving upward through kudzu and girder and air. I slip through the trapdoor into the tiny cabin, Bruce right behind me, his arms through. His head. When he's in we stand and look out.

There are windows on all sides. The glass is broken and the wind is cool and fast. The tower sways in the breeze. I can see farther and wider than I've ever seen, the sky to the west churning up in red gusts out of the distant blue trees. Across the horizon you can see the flit of lights from radio towers and smokestacks. The treetops spread below seem solid enough to walk across. It would be easy to forget what you know of the life beneath, to think of it like the bottom of the sea, a place where dark shapes move through columns of light, where schools of things drift like clouds.

Blackbirds rise from the trees and climb the sky. Bats hurtle past. Turning, I can see the sun disappearing into the treetops, the western landscape rimming with red, a stain spreading up, out, like blood, the sky darkening into pinholes of light.

"This reminds me," Bruce says, and he tells about a night he spent in Vietnam. They were south of the DMZ, a listening post, he and a buddy shoulder to shoulder in a foxhole they'd dug. Nothing happening. So dark, not even stars that night. Whispering. Bruce telling his friend what he'd be doing if he were at home. What? the friend said. Be at the drive-in with my girlfriend, Bruce said. Would you have popcorn? the friend asked, and Bruce said, Hell yes, buttered, and beer we smuggled in; we'd be drinking and watching the movie. What movie? the friend wanted to know. A western, Bruce said. John Wayne. I'd have my arm around her, Bruce said. And he felt his friend's arm go around him in the dark. And he put his arm around his friend, in the dark. And they talked some more, they talked all night, telling things they would do if they were home, and for a while it seemed as if they were at home, that the things they were talking about were real things, real girls and beer and cowboy movies.

After that Bruce is quiet. He looks out over the sky, he's watching the stars. He takes two of the deer legs from his pockets and holds one in each hand. He drums lightly on the windowsill with the hooves, and a metallic rhythm fills the sky, like something running, and he drums harder and faster, the walls and floor humming, pieces of glass rattling in the windows, flat echoes returning from somewhere. Noiseless flurries appear in the window and disappear: bats, lured by the vibration, brought down from the sky, drawn like deer to a baited field, like people to whatever they're drawn to.

But I'm remembering the time before, the race through the woods, the lake. Imagining what's happening there now, in those woods, the water, the cave, in that other part of the world. How it builds from inside the limestone, the tiny drumming of air and bodies that you feel on your skin rather than hear. They erupt at once from every inch of the cave. They fill the sky and blacken the water with their reflections. They pour out in a continuous stream, keep pouring out, like blood pumped from a heart. They brush your face and you sink in the water so only your eyes remain above the surface. It's like a storm, thousands and thousands of bats in the air together. Before now you didn't know there could be this much of anything at the same time, and you forget to be afraid, forget whoever's with you and where, why, who you are, forget everything except now and how the sky and the air are alive enough to touch, if only you didn't need your arms to stay afloat.

blue horses

Earl rose early and made coffee. He stood over the stove, sipping and staring out the window, where it was still dark. He could make out the dim lines of Evelyn's car, and of his truck beside the gate, and he knew Mace would be sleeping in the cab, drunk. Somebody had dropped him off last night: Earl had heard the dogs barking, the truck door slam. Shivering, he finished his coffee and rinsed the cup, left it hanging on its peg by the knife rack and went to put on his boots.

He locked the door behind him and zipped his jacket to his neck. His breath curled away in the wind as he went down the porch steps with his hands jammed in his pockets and hurried across the yard to his truck. The windshield was frosted, and when he opened the door a cowboy hat rolled out. Smell of beer. Mumbling, Earl picked up the hat and shook it off and looked at Mace in his big sheepskin coat, the heavy collar hiding all but the long black hair, his knees nothing but frayed white holes.

"Wake up, you bum," Earl said, swatting him with the hat.

Mace coughed.

Earl reached in and moved his friend's feet, the boot leather icy, then climbed in and ground the starter until the truck kicked to life.

Mace sat up and rubbed his eyes. "Time is it?"

"About five."

Mace took the cowboy hat and squared it on his head. He leaned and turned the rearview mirror and looked at himself, then turned it back, nowhere near where it was. "God almighty," he said.

Earl adjusted the mirror.

"I ain't drunk," Mace said. He took the hat off. "Okay, a little, maybe. Who can blame me?"

"How come you didn't come on in the house?"

"I seen Evelyn's car."

Earl shrugged. "You coulda came on in."

"Y'all make up?"

"You might say."

"Get you any?"

Earl looked at him.

"Whoa ho," Mace sang, "this boy's done got his tree trimmed."

"Where'd you go last night?" Earl asked.

"Judge's. Me and Hobart and them. Played a little pool, drunk a little beer, did some dancing. Won me this hat playing quarters."

By now Earl could see through the windshield and he rattled the gear and they eased past the mailbox into the road.

"Think you might pull over, get me some coffee?" Mace asked.

They stopped at the store and with the truck idling hurried across the concrete slab past the diesel tanks where a Peterbilt sat humming, its lights off. They went inside and got coffee. Earl paid, then held the door for Mace and they came out sipping at their steaming cups.

In the truck, Mace put the cowboy hat on his knee and fiddled with the heater knobs. "We getting Jimmyboy?"

"Got to. He's got the gun."

There was little traffic on the causeway and Earl drove in silence. He shook a cigarette from his pack and offered the pack to Mace. Mace got one with shaky fingers and lit it with the truck's lighter, then lit Earl's. They smoked and looked out their windows at the gas stations just opening for the day and at the bait shops that never closed. A few blacks were already fishing along the rails of the bridges, coat hoods up and bursts of breath appearing like Morse code. In the distance the smokestacks from the paper mill and chemical plants blinked warnings against low-flying aircraft.

After a while Mace cleared his throat. "She gonna stay this time?"

"Don't know."

"She say when she's leaving?"

Earl shook his head.

"How come Mike can't get his own damn pistol?" Mace asked.

"If he can't even drive a car anymore," Earl said, "you think they'd let him have a gun?"

They crossed the bridge with the river underneath and the mill to their right and rode down the hill into Mobile. There were condemned buildings, and paralleling the highway were railroad tracks with strings of empty boxcars. The ones with closed doors would have transients sleeping in them. Earl turned left and crossed the tracks.

They entered a trailer park with rusty cars in every yard and sleepy-looking dogs emerging from under the trailers, barking halfhearted steam. Behind a seedy double-wide Earl saw three blacks standing around a smoking barrel, stamping their feet and passing a paper bag back and forth between them. The names of the streets were biblical: Matthew, Mark, Luke, John. Earl put his cigarette in his mouth and turned left onto John. Jimmyboy lived at the end of the road, in the trailer of some woman he'd taken up with.

They left the truck chugging and got out and hurried across the dirt yard. On the steps they both pounded on the door, a draft reaching up at them from under the trailer and stinging their dry legs.

"Wake up, you dickweed," Mace said through his teeth.

A light flared in the rear of the trailer, then disappeared. They heard footsteps down the hall and Jimmyboy frowned at them through the window.

"Hang on," he said.

The handle clicked and the door swung in, Jimmyboy holding a flashlight, standing behind it with an army blanket on his bony shoulders. They brushed past him and stood in a tight circle in the dark room.

"Where's your damn lights?" Mace asked.

"Storm come through while ago," Jimmyboy said. "Knocked the juice out."

"There ain't been no storm," Mace said. "Y'all just ain't paid your power bill."

"You ready?" Earl asked.

"Naw, man, I ain't going."

"The hell you mean 'ain't going'?"

Jimmyboy turned off the flashlight. "My old lady, she say it ain't right."

"Bullshit," Mace said. "You're going if I have to drag your skinny black ass."

"Jesus," Earl said. "Well, did you get the gun at least?"

"Man, you not serious?"

A voice from the back of the trailer silenced them. "Jimmy?"

"It's okay, baby," he called. "Man, y'all got to go," he whispered. "Albertha find out who I'm talking to, she'll get her razor."

"*Jimmyboy?*"

"I'm coming, baby."

Earl said, "Have you got the goddamn pistol?"

Jimmyboy left and they heard a drawer open, then close. Earl felt the gun, heavy and cold, pushed into his hands.

"We'll see you," he said.

"Some fucking friend," Mace added.

He opened the door and cold air swirled in. He went out first and as Earl followed, he felt Jimmyboy's hand on his shoulder, but he went on down the steps after Mace. They got into the truck. It had started raining; you could see it on the windshield and past the windshield Jimmyboy standing in the door. Earl put the truck in reverse and backed out. They held their cups and sipped at them while Earl drove slowly past the grumbling dogs and over the oyster shells and across the railroad tracks and past the deserted buildings and boarded-up windows and rusting box-cars.

The pistol on the seat between them.

"Is it loaded?" Earl asked.

Mace picked it up and ejected the clip, then pushed it back in. "Yeah."

They rode, had each smoked another cigarette before Mace said, "You know what I just remembered? Tomorrow's Christmas Eve. You think Mike realized that?"

Earl didn't say anything.

"Couple of weeks ago I seen him in Food World," Mace went

on. "Went up to him and said, 'Howdy, Mike, how you doing?' And Mike, he says, 'Not bad for a dead man.' That's a hell of a thing to say, ain't it? You're trying to act normal and he pulls that shit on you."

Mace was holding the pistol. "Fuck, it's cold," he said.

They went back through the tunnel and over the causeway, past the fishermen and the seagulls that stood on the concrete railing or perched on light poles. They went under the Bayway.

When they passed Argiro's Store, Mace looked back over his shoulder. "Did you see that?"

"What?"

"That damn midget. He was putting air in a tire. Not even squatting down, just sorta bent over like."

They got out in Mike's yard. He lived in woods with no neighbors for a half-mile. The rain was gone, leaving a dewy mist that stung their faces as they looked at each other across the hood of the truck. The sky, seen in patches through the trees, was starting to pale.

"It's good luck to see a midget," Mace said.

The line of windows across the front of Mike's house glowed, as if he'd gone from room to room turning on lights. The front door stood open.

They saw him. Through one of the windows, in one of the rooms. Walking. He appeared in another window and disappeared. Earl reached into the truck and got the pistol. He slipped it into his coat pocket. He took one last drag on his cigarette and dropped it into the frost. Mace did likewise. With their hands in their pockets they walked across the yard, past the frozen birdbath, past a shovel standing upright in the earth. Mike's dog looked out the door, and wagging its wire of a tail trotted to the edge of the porch and jumped off and came sideways toward them. Its ears flattened as Mace bent to rub its muzzle and allow himself to be licked in the face. His and the dog's breath mingled, and Earl waited as Mace said soft quiet words that only the dog heard. When Mace stood and they went up the steps, the dog stayed in the yard.

Earl rapped on the doorjamb but got no answer. Knocking the muddy ice from their boots, they stepped into the living room. There was no furniture, not even curtains. Mike's wife and the kids were long since gone; he'd scared them off. Mace stopped and put his red fingers into a fist mark in the paneling. He pursed his lips.

They heard a toylike whistle from the back of the house and exchanged a glance. Mace shook his head and shrugged, walked back outside. Earl watched him cross the porch and sit on the steps without looking around. The dog nosed up to him and Mace took its face in his hands.

Earl turned and went alone down the hall. Cigarette butts lay on the carpet, filters smashed into black smudges.

The whistle again.

He saw Mike sitting in the den, on a stool at the table before his model train. When Mike had worked at the mill with Earl and Mace and Jimmyboy, they had stood in this room together and eaten barbecued ribs and drunk beer and watched the train circling the tracks. There were women in the next room; you could hear their pleasant voices in the air, and outside the sound of children.

Earl cleared his throat and Mike looked around. His left eye was sewn shut. Earl had heard he'd gotten a sliver in his eye, and since he couldn't feel anything on that half of his face, he hadn't noticed until it was too late. It was one of the things a brain tumor could do.

"Hey, Mike," Earl said.

Mike wore his camouflage coat and a stocking cap. Earl went to the corner of the table and put his fingers on the cold wood and he and Mike watched the train go around.

Dirt and grass spread across the table had made it a miniature landscape, like the view from a fire tower. There were rocks the size of footballs that were like mountains to the train that passed them and sped around the track into what became a town—little buildings made of wood and cardboard, a block of two- and three-story buildings with windows cut out and names of stores penciled on signs, a barber shop with a striped pole, a Western Auto with a row of toy bicycles before it. There were streets of packed dirt and stoplights and stop signs and light poles strung with fishing line. There were Matchbox cars. On the outskirts of town was a forest of weeds and twigs like tiny trees, and then the rock mountains, and beyond the mountains there were more trees. At the edge of the forest was a white church with a steeple, and beside the church a graveyard with a spiked fence.

Earl studied the train as it passed through the town without stopping, as it shot over a railroad crossing. The black engine was old-timey, with a smokestack and a large cowcatcher. The coal car behind it held black pebbles and another hauled twigs whittled to resemble logs. There was a tank car, a boxcar, a passenger car. A red caboose.

"They don't use cabooses any more," Mike said. "Used to have a fellow with a walkie-talkie rode on it, that was his whole job."

Earl watched. On the edge of town the train passed a ranch: a barn and house, a windmill, a tractor. A row of pens held toy cattle and in a toothpick corral were plastic horses, the kind you buy in a bag. Some were bucking and others were calm. Inch-high pewter cowboys stood around the fence, watching. Then something caught Earl's eye.

"You got you a blue one in there," he said, pointing to the corral, to the horse that stood a little taller than the rest.

"That's my stallion," Mike said. "It's what them cowboys are talking about. He come from out past the mountains over yonder. The caboose man saw him and they went caught him."

Earl nodded, digging his hands in his pockets, imagining the cowboys going after the blue stallion. They would choose their fastest horses, he thought, and pick the best roper from among them to lead the chase. They would rise before dawn and slip quietly out of their barns with shouldered saddles, smoking cig-arettes and laughing nervously. They knew a blue stallion would mean a dangerous chase of speed and dust and jumps and ducking of tree limbs like thick arms swatting at you as the earth thun-dered by. A chase that might go for miles, hours. The blue stallion ahead at a full gallop, losing the cowboys one by one to fatigue or injury or death, until at last the only cowboy is the roper, a young man with short hair and a tan face, his hat beating against his shoulders, spurs bloody, a tall young man with a pretty wife at home asleep, a wife whose thighs he parted the night before, who held him knowing of his dangerous morning race. With her lips open and her eyes closed as he moves over her, she is thinking of him on his horse, his head low, sweat streaming in muddy tracks down his skin. She sees the blue stallion before him and his fist rising and circling and the loop rising in the air over him, lashing from his open palm at the straining stallion and settling over its neck, its flowing blue mane, its frothy nostrils and teeth, its wide glaring eyes.

"Never rode a train when I was a boy," Mike said. "Now none of 'em have cabooses."

The train whistled as it passed the farm and turned with the track.

"Listen," Earl said, "I gotta go. We're late for work."

He stood a moment, watching Mike watch the train, then he slipped the gun out of his pocket and set it on the table, near the church.

Mace and the dog sat in the truck, waiting. When Earl shut his door, the dog got up and turned circles until Mace made it lie down and put its head in his lap. "Shhh," he said. Earl lit his last cigarette, and smoking it, drove through the woods and out to the highway and soon pulled onto the causeway. The early morning traffic was thickening, cars headed to work starting to turn off their lights.

Mace hugged himself. "Don't your damn heater work?"

They took a right and got on the bridge. Over the rail the mill glowed in the fog like something that had risen smoking from the depths and now sat seething and wracked there, among the ruins.

"I'm freezing to death," Mace said.

For Randall Duke

the ballad of duane juarez

Ned uses dynamite to fish with. They come swirling to the top, stunned and stupid. You lean over the rail of Ned's expensive boat and scoop them. You drink his beer and smoke his grass. Stay out all night and lie to your wife. Sometimes Ned brings girls, and we know from experience that the moon on the water and the icy Corona from Ned's live wells and the right Jimmy Buffett song on the CD make Ned's girls drip like sponges. You can crawl inside these soft wet girls that Ned finds and sleep there all night. They're intelligent, Ned's girls. They read novels. They're real estate brokers or paralegals or college students.

Where does Ned find these girls?

He's rich. They find him.

I've done the boat thing with Ned like four times, but I'm not rich. In fact I'm poor. I don't shave but I do drink too much and sometimes in the evening I throw moldy fruit through the windows of the house Ned lets me rent, one-fifty a month, though I can't remember the last time I paid. Ned understands. He buys *Playboy* magazines and looks through them once, then gives them to me. That's what it's like to be rich.

Here's what it's like to be poor. Your wife leaves you because you can't find a job because there aren't any jobs to find. You empty the jar of pennies on the mantel to buy cigarettes. You hate to answer the phone; it can't possibly be good news. When your friends invite you out, you don't go. After a while, they stop inviting. You owe them money, and sometimes they ask for it. You tell them you'll see what you can scrape up.

Which is this: nothing.

If you're wondering what somebody like Ned's doing with somebody like me, it's because he's my little brother. I married for love, Ned married for money. Now he pays my light bill; it's in his wife Nina's name. Ned'll come by on Thanksgiving or Christmas day with a case of beer, and he leaves what we don't finish, maybe two cans. He rents movies which we watch on a TV/VCR unit from his real estate office.

In the divorce my ex got everything. Even kept her composure—no crying in front of the judge for her. That was somebody else's department. Thank God there weren't any kids: that's what Ned said. I came home from fishing one morning and she was gone, the damn house empty. I called Ned from a gas station because she'd taken our telephones.

"Bitch ripped off everything except the mallards and the deer heads," I said.

"Well," Ned said, "buck up, big bro. Some people don't have that much."

So what Ned does now is find me these jobs. I cut the grass around some of his rental houses, rake the dead leaves, use the Weed Whacker. I wash his Porsche twice a week when the pollen's thick, and this one time he even let me drive it to get it tuned. In the rearview mirror, I looked like Ned. But it was my eyebrow poking up over his sunglasses and it was me smoking his cigars from the dash pocket and shifting without using the clutch.

It was me, Duane, cruising past the downtown hookers standing in their heels to see if there was something in my price range.

Another time Ned let me clean out the attic of a foreclosure, he said keep anything I wanted. Here's what I took: three shotguns, two graphite fishing rods, a tent, a rocking horse, a road atlas, an ice chest, a coin collection, a Styrofoam boulder from one of Nina's plays. When Ned asked if I found anything worth keeping I went, "Not really." I used the coin collection to buy TV dinners and pawned the rest, except for one of the shotguns, a nice Ithaca twelve-gauge pump.

It's been a year since Debra left and I'm still in the getting-over-it stage. I'm drunk every day; that helps. With the TV Ned left I discovered *My Three Sons* and soap operas and PBS. At night I sit and watch. There was this show called *Animals Are Beautiful People*. It was funny as hell. This baboon in the middle of a field picks up a rock looking for something to eat and there's a snake coiled there. The baboon screams, then faints dead away. When he wakes a few minutes later, he picks up the same rock, and there's the snake and whammo, the goddamn baboon faints again.

One night Ned calls. "Hey, big bro, Nina wants to sell the house."

He means the one I'm living in. Holding the remote, the TV muted, I look around.

"But hey, don't panic," Ned says. "The price she wants, they'll never move it. You'll just have this for-sale sign in your yard.

"But you might need to cut that grass once in a while," he says. "You can borrow our lawn mower.

"Another thing," he says. "We're going to the Bahamas for a

couple weeks. Will you check up on our place while we're gone? Just drive by a few times, make sure it hasn't burned down.

"There's some cats there, too," he says. "All those damn strays Nina feeds? Won't get 'em fixed either. Says, listen to this, that it interrupts the natural goddamn flow of everything.

"Make you a deal," Ned says. "If all those cats are gone when we get back, I'll pay the responsible party two hundred bucks. All on the Q-T, though. Nina would freak."

On the morning they're leaving for the Bahamas, I'm sleeping on the porch: it's too hot inside, and the flies.

Ned kicks a beer can.

"Hey, bro," he says.

I sit up, blink, see dried vomit on my pants. Brush at the ants working in it.

Ned tosses me a small brown paper bag. "This might come in handy," he says, and winks.

The bag's heavy, like a pint.

Ned squats and socks me in the arm. "We'll have to go fishing when I get back, huh?" He stands up, goes past the for-sale sign. Screeches off in the Porsche.

I open the bag to find a small silver pistol and two plastic boxes of twenty-two cartridges.

Ned and Nina have been gone for a week when I decide it's time to head on over there. I sit up in bed at four in the afternoon and blink at the calendar girl. Finish the beer on the nightstand. The pistol will never work on cats—they'll probably zigzag all over the place and my aim's not that good—so I dig in the closet and find the Ithaca and a box of shells—number eights, birdshot—and go outside, load the stuff into the backseat. I get in front with the pistol, not relishing the idea of all that shooting with my hangover.

There's a line of big black ants, some carrying white things over their heads, going across the dash of the car. Not to mention the water standing in the back floorboard, hatching all these mosquitoes. I put the car in gear and drive to Ned and Nina's big spread in the woods. The magnolia trees and the million-year-old oaks and the Spanish moss. All so damn depressing.

Their lawn's high; Ned'll probably ask me to mow it. I get out slapping at mosquitoes, and four or five cats eye me from the lawn furniture. One yawning from the limb of a tree. There's a sprinkler that I turn on: it makes a ticking sound that alarms the cats. The pistol is snug in my pocket and I take it out, load it. Point it at a fat calico.

"Bang," I say.

I have the house key I copied off Ned's key ring the day he let me take the Porsche. Nina, you can bet, won't like me being inside. I go up the steps, winded at the top, and let myself into the den and sit on the sofa and rest. Rustic as hell. I leaf through a magazine. Try to remember the kind of wood they use to make these big ceiling beams. I get up and wander to the kitchen and take a Heineken from the fridge, put the rest of the six-pack under my arm and start rummaging through the pantry. There's several cans of sardines and tuna that I pocket. Then I notice something else: Ned's Porsche keys hanging on a rack over the sink.

Outside, I open the cans and imitate Nina's squeaky, cute voice: "Here, kitty kitty kitty."

Soon the clueless cats are feasting and purring at my feet, rubbing their shoulders against my ankles. They're half starved. With

Ned's Porsche's trunk opened I pick up them one by one by the scruffs of their necks and load them in. They're getting wary now, making these low moaning noises.

But five cats and three kittens are locked away before the smarter ones disappear.

I let myself back into Ned's house and climb upstairs to wash my hands. I look like hell in the bathroom mirror. Those eyes, Christ. Opening the medicine cabinet, I find some Tylenol and swallow four. There's some Valium, too, and I empty most of them from the bottle into my shirt pocket. Nina's prescription. There's dozens of bottles of pills in here. Reading their names is like reading Mexican or something. I unscrew some of the caps and sniff inside. Stale. When I find a container of Nina's birth control pills it gives me a semi. A little packet of orange sinus pills looks sort of like the birth control, and I switch them.

Sometimes—and I'm not proud of this—I do a strange thing regarding Nina. I know it's embarrassing, but on nights when Ned's out, I call from a pay phone and wait for Nina to answer. When she says hello, I just hold the line, let her hear me breathing.

"I know it's you, you bitch!" she screams. "You whore!"

Then I hang up, excited and guilty.

Finishing my beer, I go past the door-length mirror into Ned and Nina's bedroom. Their water bed isn't made. I crawl in with my boots on and slosh around: Nina's pillow's sweet smell, a blond pubic hair curling on the quilt.

Going through the nightstand I find seventy-five dollars. In Nina's underwear drawer there are frilly pieces of lingerie that are like Kleenexes they're so delicate. I toss one into the air and let it land on my face. Perfume. There are little fragrant soap balls in the drawer. I lift a thin negligee from the pile and hold it in front of the mirror.

The phone rings.

I stuff the nightie in my pocket and close the drawer, hurry down to the living room where the answering machine is. It beeps and Ned's recording plays and some asshole comes on and asks about the house for sale. Call him, he says, as soon as they get in. I study the machine. A digital number changes from 12 to 13. I press the play button and listen for awhile. There are several calls, that I erase, about the house for sale.

My house.

Outside, you can hear the cats meowing and clawing around in the trunk of the Porsche. I get in and rev the engine, spin off and take curves hard and fast to shut them up.

To be honest, I don't think I've ever killed a cat. Deer, sure. Doves, squirrels, coons. Practically any game animal. Three or four dog accidents with my car and a few dozen snakes, possums and armadillos.

But none of that's the worst thing I've ever done. The worse thing I've ever done was when I woke up in my car after drinking all night with Ned—it was a time I don't remember that much, a week or two after Deb left, *blackouts* are what they call them in jail—and my clothes had a lot of blood on them. I couldn't remember where it came from, so I called Ned and he said he didn't have a clue. Said not to call him at work. Hung up on me. It was my first week renting Ned's place. There was so much blood that I burned the clothes in the fireplace, went outside wearing a bedsheet and watched the smoke coming out of the chimney, worried what my new neighbors would think of a man who burns fires in August and stands in his yard in a sheet.

While I'm paying five dollars for gas at the Jiffy Mart, the clerk squints her eyes and says, "What's that commotion coming out your trunk? Sound like you got you a wildcat in there."

I tell her it's my ex-wife and she laughs a toothless, good-natured laugh.

A drink seems in order next, so I drive the Porsche to the Key West and get a corner table. I finger the pistol in my pocket and think about killing things. Stub out my cigarette in an ashtray shaped like an oyster shell. I glance around. This place is designed to look like an island. Tropical shit, I mean. Every once in a while a fairy floats in thinking it's a gay bar because of how Key West is down in Florida. I guess they don't take the hint from the pickups in the parking lot. The gun racks in back windows. But when they see how the regulars glare at them, they get the picture pretty quick and gulp down their peppermint schnapps or whatever they drink and drop a giant tip for Juarez, the bartender. Juarez for the record isn't foreign: his real name's Larry, but Larry says with a foreign name you get more pussy. Over a shot of tequila, I consider changing my name to something better, tougher-sounding.

I roll my mind over this: What if Ned ever hires me for a real job, to knock off a person, say? Or at the least just beat the shit out of some asshole, maybe some yo-yo who cuts Ned off at a red light and Ned gets the guy's license number. Or maybe somebody's fucking Nina. Ned calling me and saying he's got a big score, yeah, the real thing. Meet him at the Key West. *"It's a doctor,"* he'll whisper in my ear, *"a fat plastic surgeon that's fucking her."*

All I'd have to do is call Ned in the middle of the night and hang up a few times. Get him worried.

"Ten grand," I'll say, and Ned'll go, "Too much," and I'm like, "Hey, Ned? Then pay somebody else, okay, Ned? This ain't some piece of real estate you're buying, Ned. Some piece of ass. This is a professional job, little bro, and if you get some clown who don't know what he's doing, he gets excited by the blood and suddenly you got a body on your hands. Now you're dealing with forensics detectives, Ned, guys pulling hairs off the body with fucking tweezers."

I'm enjoying my little plot until Juarez appears and hits me with more Cuervo. Seeing him reminds me that you need an alias for certain kinds of deals. I pronounce my name out loud and decide my last name's the problem. So I take my cue from Juarez and there on the spot become Duane Juarez. *He* sounds like a dangerous guy, somebody you don't fuck with.

I head to the bar to buy the original Juarez his poison of choice. Pouring, he wants to know what the occasion is, and I tell him I've just made an important decision and we clink our glasses.

"To you," he says. "To Duane."

"Juarez," I add.

"What?"

"Nothing."

Then the subject of cat-killing comes up, and Juarez tells me he grew up on a farm where their mousing cats were always giving birth. Juarez says his old man would stuff a whole damn litter of kittens in a croaker sack and beat it against the ground until the bag stopped moving. Which reminds me that I have a job to do, so I pay my tab with one of Ned's twenties and head outside. There's another cat sitting on the Porsche, attracted, I guess, by the noise or the cat piss smell coming from the trunk.

"Scram," I say, but this one's friendly, and as I pass, it strains its head toward me. "Nice pussy cat," I say, scratching it behind the ears. Then I take it in both hands and toss it into the bushes.

I drive to the woods, down dirt roads, leaving a trail of green bottles. Kudzu, wisteria, honeysuckle. Miles since the last house. I cross a little bridge with ivy and pull off the road into a clearing. Get out feeding shells into the belly of the twelve-gauge. The sky is high and the air is clean and clear and you can hear all these crows. I go to the trunk and open it a crack. Paws and whiskers appear and I swat at them with the gun barrel. They meow and hiss, and finally a whole cat wriggles out. It kicks off the bumper and I slam the trunk, shuck the shotgun's action and lead the cat perfectly as it goes around in circles.

I don't feel the gun's kick, but the cat jackknifes and lands and now it's only half a cat. It flops a couple of times. The woods are bone quiet, everything frozen, the leaves not rattling, the acorns perfectly still on their stobs. I go stand near the cat, which is dead now, and watch the black stuff pooling around its belly. It's a dark gray one with white feet, the kind you'd name Mittens. Some of its fur is moist with blood and I shuck the shotgun; the smoking red shell case lands beside my boot. I think this cat ought to have a name, so Mittens it is. Was.

Back at the trunk, I open the last beer and raise it in a toast, then let another cat out. It hauls ass for the trees.

"Nina!" I yell. The first shot whirls her around but doesn't stop her, and even before the gunshot's faded I've jacked in another shell and I'm batting my way through limbs and spiderwebs in the woods, following her bright red trail. I find her scrabbling up a tree with her sides pumping. When she sees me she howls with her ears flat on her head. She tries to climb higher, but with another shot I send her spread-eagled through the air and she hits the leaves like a tiny bearskin rug.

Then I remember something. It was when we were teenagers, after Ned and I had dropped Nina off from a drive-in movie one night. We both liked her and we'd been drinking and smoking grass. As Ned drove home, we saw beside the road this dead poodle that had belonged to Nina's family for like eleven years— it'd been missing for a day or two. The dog was lying on its side, its legs straight, and—Ned's idea of a joke—we took it back to Nina parents' mansion and stood it there dead on the porch, like a statue. In the car, Ned laughed so hard he started gagging. Then he passed out. When I snuck back to get the dog and bury it, Nina's father caught me in the porch light, my hands around the poodle.

I name the next cat Debra, because it's gray like one Deb used to have, but even as I pull the trigger I feel guilty. I find her wallowing in her pool of blood and shit, gnawing at her shoulder. I decide instead to hang a Mexican name on her. "Maria," I say, taking the pistol from my pocket. But just when I'm about to put Maria out of her misery, I'm struck with a memory of Debra, before we got married, when there was a shitload of love. I don't know why I think of it, but there we are, on the sofa, watching *Mad Max*. I'm getting fresh and Debra's saying okay, okay, we can fool around, but we can't *do it* because she's smack in the middle of her period. So we're kissing and groping until it gets real steamy and she's climbing all over me. Finally she rolls off and stands up, kind of swaying, her nipples hard through her shirt, and I follow her into the bedroom. She throws the covers off and gets a towel and spreads it over the bed. There's this loud zip and she steps out of her skirt. *I hope you like it rare,* she says. Closing one eye, I squeeze the trigger on Maria and that's that.

At the trunk this time two escape and my beer bottle rolls off the car. Juan the Manx heads for the woods, his body opening and closing like a little hand, and I fire and bowl him over, then shucking the pump whip around and wing—I think—the one jumping into the bushes.

Left now are the kittens, two identical blacks and one solid white. I open the trunk wide: they're cowering behind the spare. All this noise has their fur ruffled, their tails puffy, eyes red, ears flat, teeth bared. "Kitty kitty kitty," I say, and get one of the blacks by the scruff and lift it out and hold it up against the sky. Do it with the pistol right there, specks of blood on my hand and arm.

That was Leigh, one of Ned's girls, and this is Cindy, and there she goes, flung, landing in that tree. But here's Duane Juarez, reloading.

The white kitten is moving. It jumps out, disappears under the car, and here's Duane Juarez dropping to his knees, watching the kitten scramble up into the engine. Duane Juarez on his belly, sliding under the car, and trying to nab the bastard getting bit hard on the knuckle.

Duane Juarez by the Dumpster in the alley behind the Key West, kicking a stranger in the chest. Picking the guy up and breaking his nose with a head butt, Ned behind them, rooting in the shadows. Duane Juarez picking a tooth out of his knuckle and tossing it to Ned for a souvenir.

The woods are as quiet as a back alley. There's only one way to deal with this kind of cat situation. You have to get in the

Porsche and rev its engine to a scream. You have to leave the shotgun barrel holding down the accelerator. You have to climb onto the car with the pistol. The hood might buckle with your weight, but it's your job to stand there, ready.

This one's Ned.

a tiny history

Paul and Prissy are coming to play spades. We're having them over because they had us over a few weeks ago. Jan and I had a swell time there. It's been a rocky year for Paul, but Prissy has taken him back and dropped the charges—he tried to set fire to her bar—on the conditions that he (A) stop drinking and (B) enroll at the community college. Jan thought higher education was something I ought to try, too. She said it might give our own shaky marriage a solid leg to stand on. So now Paul and I are in this Saturday morning public speaking class together.

"*Pubic* speaking," Paul calls it.

Our wives arranged the game of spades at Paul and Prissy's. Jan and I arrived at their house on Dauphin Island at six-thirty. We ate at eight, then brought out the cards at about nine. I'd never played, but spades is a pretty straightforward game and I caught on fairly quickly, though Paul and I—versus the girls— lost. But the thing was, we all had such a blast that we didn't finish till seven the next morning, after eight pots of coffee and, for Paul and Jan, several packs of cigarettes. Paul was on the wagon, so none of us drank. The other thing was, I had to be at work at the chemical plant that evening at four.

So one night last week I ran into Paul at a liquor store. He was drinking again. He was buying some rum and I was buying some beer and we got to talking about what a swell time we'd had playing spades that night, so I invited him and Prissy over to our house the next Saturday night. He said it sounded good, what should they bring?

Jan loved the idea, too. She called Prissy and told them to arrive at seven. "Don't bring anything except yourselves," she said. "Let us handle everything."

Jan was actually excited. We'd been married less than a year and hadn't really had anybody over. Not even our parents. (It's been kind of iffy around here, with the baby and all.) Jan vacuumed the entire house—we're renting—and washed the walls and rearranged the living room furniture. We're broke, so she went to her mother's and borrowed another fifty bucks and bought the ingredients for chicken piccata. She also got four bottles of white wine—Paul was off the wagon, after all—and a deck of cards.

Paul and I had Pubic Speaking the morning of the Saturday they were supposed to come over. We have to make a speech every week, and that day we were doing demonstration speeches. I was going to show how to put on a gas mask, which we use for emergency getaways at the plant, and I needed a volunteer to wear the mask while I delivered the speech. Paul offered to help with mine if I'd help with his. I asked what he was demonstrating, and he said he planned to show how to perform—get this—an emergency tracheotomy.

When the class started, Paul went first. He stood and made his way to the front of the room. He cleared his throat and said, "Imagine you're in a restaurant and that man"—he pointed to me—"starts choking." I blushed. Paul motioned for me to come stand in front of him.

"The first thing you'd do if he's choking," Paul said, "is to perform the Heimlich maneuver. You put your arms around his stomach like so, and put your thumbs here, in the soft spot."

His arms were around me, his thumbs in my solar plexus.

"To dislodge whatever's choking him," he said, "you apply a quick punch of pressure, like so." He jammed his thumbs into my soft spot and pushed all the air out of me. I felt dizzy, like I'd been hit.

"But what if there's an obstruction?" Paul asked. "Something preventing that bit of food from being dislodged?" He let me go. "Then what would you do?"

Nobody said anything.

"In that case," Paul said, "you'd need to perform an emergency tracheotomy. To do this, you want the victim lying on his back."

"Or her," someone in the audience said—it's a very politically correct class.

"Right," Paul said, grinning. "Or *her* back." He has this way of making things sound dirty.

As rehearsed, Paul and I moved the overhead projector and slid the table to the center of the room. I climbed onto the table, my legs hanging over the edge.

"What you do," Paul said, "is hold the victim here"—he placed his hand under my chin—"and make sure he—or *she*—is unconscious."

I closed my eyes.

"Now," Paul said, "the first thing you do is find the Adam's apple. Then you follow the victim's throat down until you locate a soft spot. That's where you'll make your incision."

The audience was quiet. No sound in the room except Paul's watch, ticking at my throat.

"Of course a sterilized scalpel's best," Paul said, "only almost nobody carries sterilized scalpels in their shirt pockets." Polite laughter. "But," Paul went on, "lots of people do carry pocket-knives."

I cracked an eye. The knife Paul flicked open was seven inches long, its blade stained and worn, as if it'd been used to skin animals and cut wire and slash Prissy's tires, which was another thing Paul had done the night he tried to set her bar afire.

"You put the tip of the blade on the soft spot, like so," Paul said.

Its cold steel point touched my throat.

"After the knife's in place," Paul said, "you hit it flat, with the palm of your hand, like so." His hand rose, had just started back down when I shut my eyes.

Nothing happened. I peeked and Paul was explaining how you might need to stick a pen or drinking straw in the bloody hole like so, so I could breathe through it. When he finished, the audience clapped, and I got up and went to my seat, sweaty and nervous. Later, my speech was okay. I got a 78, ten points less than Paul.

I bought gas on the Texaco card on the way home. I added a quart of oil, put a six-pack on the card, too. At home, Jan was asleep. I took off my shoes and crawled into bed beside her and slid my hand inside her panties.

"Don't," she said without turning over.

"Fine." I went into the living room and watched TV and drank the six-pack, fell asleep on the sofa.

Jan had set the alarm clock for five P.M. I sat up. She was already in the kitchen, banging things around. She sent me to the Jiffy Mart for a bag of ice. When I came back, she was taking a bath. I walked in and sat on the toilet and talked to her. She lay in the water, listening to me tell about having the knife at my throat. Then she sat up, a drop of water hanging from her left nipple.

"Wanna fuck?" I asked.

"They'll be here any minute," she said.

Half an hour later I'm at the table working on next week's speech (persuasive) when their little VW rattles up outside. I hear them get out, arguing, and walk to the door. I let them in.

Paul's a tall man, taller than me. Bald, bearded. Red eyes. Once, at a party at Prissy's bar, he made a pass at Jan. It was before we were married, before he and Prissy split for the first time. Prissy and I were mixing shots at the bar, and Jan and Paul were dancing, and he grabbed the cheeks of her ass and stuck his tongue in her ear, saying sex and marriage were totally different concoctions.

Prissy's half-Vietnamese. She's short and dark, has thick lips. Sexy. If you look closely enough at her fine black hair, you can see through it to the brown skin of her head. We have a tiny history, the two of us, that nobody knows about. A kiss, a long time ago. It tasted like tequila.

Jan comes in from the kitchen and we all say our hellos, sit and chat for a while. Then Jan says she'll finish dinner. Prissy offers to help and they go, leaving Paul and me alone on the sofa. I tell him he scared the shit out of me with that knife and he laughs, lighting a cigarette. I ask him if he wants a before-dinner cocktail and he says he thought I'd never ask. I go into the kitchen and get a bottle of wine and, using the corkscrew, work the cork out. I pour us two glasses and head back to the living room. The bottle comes with me. Paul is standing, examining Jan's bronze sculpture of the pregnant woman on her perch over the television. She—the statue—is about a foot tall, and I love her perfectly rounded, sensuous belly.

"Who made that?" Paul wants to know.

"Jan. In art school."

"Damn." He takes the glass I offer.

"She's for sale," I say.

We sip, eye the pregnant lady.

"How much?" Paul asks. "Not cheap, I bet."

"You'll have to ask the artist." It sounds more sarcastic than I mean it to.

"Bet she'd cost a small mint," he says. "Christ, she's beautiful." He reaches a finger out, touches her breast.

"Paul," I say, glancing toward the kitchen.

"Nice tits," he says.

"Can I talk to you?"

"Hell, yeah." He takes out his cigarettes, taps the pack against his palm.

"How often"—I lower my voice—"do you and Prissy, you know, do it?"

He closes one eye while he lights a cigarette.

I raise my hand. "If it's too personal . . ."

"No," he says. "I'd guesstimate about three, four times a week. More during the holidays. Vacations. Why?"

I finish my wine. "Jan and I, we hardly ever do it."

In the kitchen, the girls laugh.

"Jesus," Paul says. "Y'all've only been married what, two years?"

"Eight or nine months."

"Jesus. When me and Prissy first got married, we did it every night for like the first year."

"If it was up to me," I say, refilling my glass, "so would we. But Jan's frigid or something. I don't know. She never gets horny. If it was up to her, we'd never do it."

"Jesus."

"Even on our honeymoon. She was still pissed about my bachelor party, so then I get pissed and go, 'You wanna just skip it?' and she's like, 'No, we ought to consummate.' Shit. What a word. 'Consummate.' "

I drain my glass. Paul finishes his, too, and I pour us more.

"With Prissy it's something about how she was brought up," he says. "I don't think she's ever turned me down. Even if we're throwing ashtrays and picture frames at each other all afternoon, once we hit that bed, boom. She'll do anything."

"Anything?"

His eyebrows go up. "Name it."

"How long have y'all been married?"

He thinks. "Nine years?"

We don't say anything. You can hear the girls chattering in the kitchen.

Then I say, "Jan claims it has to do with losing the baby. . . . She says it'll get better. That I have to be patient."

"Yeah, that was probably tough on her. How long's it been?"

"Like three months. But I'm not sure it's just that. I think she's really frigid and this gives her an excuse. Hell, even when she does let me, she just lies there. Won't even put her arms around me. Never says anything. I'll be like, 'Want to?' And sometimes, if she went shopping and bought new shoes or something, she'll go, 'Okay,' and follows me into the bedroom and drops her panties and gets on the bed and goes, 'Do it.' "

"Have a drink," Paul says.

I fill my glass to its rim, then fill his. "Cheers," I say.

"I wish I knew—cheers—what to tell you."

I laugh. "What I wanted you to tell me was that you and Prissy never do it, either. At least then we'd be normal. Shit. It kills me that there're women out there who do it, who enjoy it, who *initiate* it!" I look toward the kitchen. "I'd give a hundred bucks for a blowjob."

Paul grins. "Tell Prissy. She needs a new jukebox for the bar."

The bottle is empty. We go into the kitchen for another one.

"You rascals take it easy on that wine," Jan says. "It's gotta last us all night."

"Not to fear," Paul says, lifting his glass. "Me and Prissy disobeyed your orders and brought a little something. It's in the car."

"You're so bad," Jan says, smiling.

"Paul's idea," Prissy says flatly. She turns and faces the counter, begins to cut up something. Her ass is round, nice.

Paul heads for the door. "I'll be right back."

"I'll help," I say.

Outside, with Paul's car's trunk opened, I say, "You mean you just ask, and she lets you?"

"I don't even ask. Just start rubbing her tits." He gets three bottles of red wine from a box in the trunk.

"Does she, you know, make noises?"

"Hoo boy. She's a wild thang. She likes it on rugs, chairs, tables."

"Shit." I take one of the bottles.

"Prissy would kill us both if she knew I told you that."

"I'll trade you, even money, Jan for Prissy."

"Don't tempt me," Paul says. "No matter what you hear, sex ain't everything."

"Don't bullshit me, Paul."

He slams the trunk. "Would I do that?"

We walk back into the kitchen, where Jan is dicing onions. We all laugh as she dramatically wipes a tear. Prissy smiles, standing against the counter, a glass of wine in her small hand. She sips. I stare at her until she catches me and I look away. Jan's talking about how much she misses her art school days. How now there's never enough money for her to sculpt.

"How much will you take for the pregnant chick?" I ask her. She looks at me. "Seven hundred?"

"Hoo boy," Paul says. "Go look at it, hon."

I offer Prissy my arm. "I'll show you the way, madam."

We go into the living room. Prissy's short so I have to get the pregnant lady down for her.

"Careful," I say. "She weighs a ton."

Prissy takes the statue. She examines it, runs her tiny dark fingers over the lady's belly, her thighs, her bottom, her unsmiling face.

"It weighs about twenty-five pounds," she says—she has a slight accent. "I'm a lifter." She flexes her bicep for me to feel.

I linger a squeeze on the hard muscle. "Wow."

She hands me the statue and I replace it, and without a prop we're suddenly shy and aware. We look at each other for a moment, and I know we're thinking the same thing. "We should have coffee sometime," I say. She shrugs. "Coffee. Sure." Then we go back to the kitchen. Paul's opening another bottle of wine and Jan's tasting something from a big pot. You can tell they've been laughing.

I ask Jan what the pregnant lady weighs.

"Oh. Twenty-seven pounds," she says.

"You were close," I tell Prissy.

She flexes at me.

Jan claps her hands. "Anybody hungry?"

I turn down the lights and Jan lights tall candles on the table. I put Tom Waits on the stereo. We eat the chicken, the glazed carrots, the salad and store-bought bread. Everybody raves, and Paul demands that Jan give Prissy the carrot recipe.

After dinner, Paul and I face each other, partners, and Jan and Prissy face each other. The boys against the girls. Jan gets our new playing cards, removes the cellophane and takes the jokers from the deck.

Paul says, "New cards, hmmm."

I smile and open one of Paul's bottles.

Prissy shuffles, deals. I bid two. Jan bids three, Paul four and Prissy one.

"Prissy's sandbagging," Paul says, lighting a cigarette. According to him, Prissy always bids for less than she can win. Jan lights a cigarette, too. I help myself to more wine. I'm feeling loose and warm.

We go through a few hands, nothing spectacular, then we start telling jokes. Jan gets the ball rolling with the old Why-is-six-afraid-of-seven? that I've heard a thousand times.

"You got me," Paul says, drinking.

"Why?" Prissy asks.

"Because seven ate nine!"

Everybody laughs.

Then Prissy tells her favorite: "What's the difference between parsley and pussy?"

Paul's heard it a million times, he says.

Jan and I say we don't know.

"You don't eat parsley," Prissy says.

I spit out some wine, which cracks Paul up. He has the funniest laugh—he actually goes, "Ha ha ha," like a comic-book character.

Under the table, Prissy's foot brushes mine.

We play more spades. Prissy sandbags. The cards are cut, shuffled, dealt, more jokes told—longer ones that I won't be able to remember later. I turn the radio to the oldies station and we switch to poker, bring out our dimes and nickels, go through a few games, dealer's choice.

Paul looks over his fan of cards. "Let me ask y'all something."

"Ask us anything," Jan says.

" 'Cause I'll tell anything back," he says, ha ha ha. He stops and lights a cigarette, then holds his lighter for Jan. "How can somebody have absolutely no ambition?"

Jan and I glance at each other. The room gets quiet.

"He's talking about me," Prissy says. "He always goes off on this when he's drunk."

"And I am drunk," he says.

"Yes, you are," Prissy says.

"I wouldn't say she has no ambition," I say. "She owns a bar. She's a wife. And just look at those biceps."

She grins.

"Well, take me," says Paul. "I got a day job, but it's not enough. So I play the stock market a little bit. A few investments. I tend bar on the weekends. And now I'm taking this goddamn pubic speaking class. And when I'm doing my homework, where can you find Prissy? Watching TV."

"I'm happy watching TV," she says.

"Being happy, that's all that matters," I say.

"But I'm not happy," Paul says.

"That's your problem," Jan says. "I think Prissy's right."

"But shouldn't she try to improve herself all she can?" Paul asks.

Prissy shuffles the deck. "You're talking about me like I'm not here."

"You're not," Paul says. "You're watching the fucking TV all the time."

"Paul," Prissy says, "you wouldn't even be in that goddamn class if I wasn't making you go."

"All I'm saying"—he blows smoke from his nose—"is that somebody ought to do all they can to improve theirself."

"Sure," I tell them. "To a point."

"To what point?" Paul says.

I don't say anything. Instead I pour another glass of wine. We're down to Paul's last bottle.

"All I know," he says, looking sadly at me, "is that if I had to choose between a horny, happy couch potato who watches every goddamn sitcom on the tube, who tapes fucking soap operas, and somebody who can do that"—he points to Jan's pregnant lady—"I'd choose the statue. Even if she was frigid. Goddamn," he says, "sex ain't everything."

"Paul," Prissy says, "you're embarrassing me."

"You're embarrassing *me*," Jan says, giving me this cold look.

"What?" I say.

"Deal the fucking cards, Prissy," Paul says. "Everybody ante up."

We play a few more hands, pretty much in silence. Jan won't look at me. Prissy deals a hand of five-card stud that I win with a full house. I deal a game of baseball that Jan wins with five jacks. Paul belches and says he's folding and goes to the sofa. He flicks open his knife and begins to dig at his fingernails.

Jan gets up and hurries into our bedroom, closes the door.

"Excuse me," I tell Prissy, and follow Jan.

She's lying on the bed, face in the pillow.

"You have guests," I say. "Some hostess."

"You told Paul, didn't you?" She still won't look at me.

"Course not. It's our problem."

"It's *your* problem."

I raise my voice. "What about that marriage counseling? Remember that guy saying it's not you against me, but it's us against the problem? What about that? How come this isn't us against us?"

In the other room, the television comes on.

"Oh, God," Jan says, her face hidden.

I stand over her for five minutes, until the clock says 2:18 A.M. and my head stops spinning. Now I've even lost my buzz. I go out the door, back into the living room, close the door. Paul's asleep on the sofa, his mouth open. There's a movie about Alaska on TV. Two guys cracking whips on dogsleds, crossing the frozen earth.

Prissy is at the table, playing solitaire. I see that she's gotten Paul's knife away from him. It's lying opened on the table by her elbow. She looks at me. I look back at her.

"Deal me in," I say.

dinosaurs

On the day he saw the rhinoceros, Steadman woke an hour before dawn. In the living room, in the dark, he stared at the fish tank for so long his coffee grew cold. Something, the end of a dream maybe, nagged him, left him uncertain and pensive. The house seemed too small, so he loaded his equipment and left early. Soon the knobby buckshot tires of his truck were humming comfortably along the interstate, Mobile behind him, Montgomery far ahead, the gas station signs at every exit colorful smudges in the fog.

He drove a company pickup, a big silver Ford F-250 with four-wheel-drive he rarely had to use. On the back glass he'd attached a Greenpeace decal. He knew the gas-guzzling truck and the sticker contradicted each other, but Steadman had been at odds with himself lately, a bit distracted. He nearly missed his exit, for example, and had to jab his brakes and swerve. Soon he found himself on a quiet, unfamiliar two-lane with the eight o'clock sun hazy over the trees. Where had the miles gone? Lines of barbed wire, red-tailed hawks on fence posts, cattle licking dark salt blocks. Occasionally he'd pass a rusty harrow, kudzu climbing its spikes, and think of his father, a retired geologist who loved refurbishing antique tractors. Now, in a nursing home, he called Steadman more and more but remembered him less and less.

Kilpatrick's Sinclair station was a flat gray cinder-block lump with a shed against the back and a faded green sign. Beside two antique gas pumps stood the rhinoceros, giant head lowered, right front foot lifted as if it were pawing the ground. Its purpose, Steadman guessed, was to attract customers. But from the looks of this dump the rhino might soon be out of a job.

Like you, pal, Steadman thought, watching old Kilpatrick suck on his unfiltered Camel and glower through drugstore reading glasses at the paperwork Steadman had spread across the office desk. Above them, also glowering, was a dusty crow nailed to a piece of driftwood.

"Get to it," the old man said. "I ain't got all day." Even his breath smelled like gasoline.

"Your underground tanks," Steadman began, "where you store your fuel—"

"I know what they are."

Steadman unfolded a pamphlet that explained corrosion in simple terms. "Did you know they've probably been leaking for years?"

Kilpatrick stubbed out his cigarette in a clamshell ashtray. He lit another and smoked while Steadman gave his usual pitch, how the storage tanks needed a leak detection system or, according to federal regulations, there'd be no choice but to shut down the station. At best, if the tanks were secure, leak detection wells could be installed for around a grand. At worst, Kilpatrick's tanks would have to be excavated and replaced with new EPA-approved above-ground units, a cost of several thousand dollars. When Steadman finished there was a long silence, which he finally broke with his usual remark about doing good for the environment.

"The environment?" Kilpatrick snatched off his glasses. "Take you a good long look out the window yonder at the *environment*."

Steadman gathered his papers, politely, and closed his briefcase. Outside, the hot white sky, the two-lane blacktop, the distant pine trees. No house or building in sight. Just the rhinoceros, baking in the sun.

When Steadman returned two days later—he always gave customers time to check his background—Kilpatrick was smoking and leaning against the rhinoceros with his arms folded. He wore baggy coveralls black with oil.

What he'd do first, Steadman explained, unloading his hand auger, was dig holes around the underground tanks, for soil samples. "I'll go down a few feet," he said, "and that's where we'll find your contamination."

The auger—stainless steel, extendable to twelve feet—was warm from sunlight.

Kilpatrick squinted at the corkscrew blades. "You plan to dig with that thing? By hand?"

Steadman shouldered the auger. "You want to show me where your tanks are buried?"

Kilpatrick nodded toward the right side yard of the station, then limped over the concrete and went into the glassed office and eased himself into a folding chair. Steadman watched him open the Coke machine and fan the cool air into his collar, then draw a Budweiser from the rack and pry off the lid with a bottle opener from his coveralls pocket.

Around the building was a jungle of grass, bitterweed and briars out of which stuck two four-inch-diameter pipes with padlocked caps: the ports used for measuring and filling the underground tanks. Steadman leaned the auger against the wall and walked over and gave each pipe a solid kick. He knelt and sniffed them, then took hold of the left one and started working

107

it back and forth. After a minute he had the pipe wiggling, and soon it came out of the dirt in his hands—a foot-long length not connected to anything. He tossed it in the air and caught it. Kilpatrick wasn't the first station owner to pull something like this. They'd do anything to knock him off the scent, and their bullshit usually helped subdue his guilt at closing them down.

Steadman dropped the pipe, collected the auger and walked behind the building, past a rusty trailer and the rickety shed. The dirt back here was stained with oil—Kilpatrick could be fined if Steadman chose to report him. Greasy shapes lay scattered about, transmission housings caked with grime, torque converters, leaky oil filters and stacks of cracked car batteries. There was an old bathtub full of greenish water and an anvil with a dog skull on it.

On the other side of the station Steadman kicked away a milk crate to reveal two rusty ports, the real ones, locked with combination locks. He chose a spot a few feet east and took hold of the auger's T-shaped handle and began twisting. The ground was hard, rocky, but Steadman's arms were hard, too, his skin brown from digging hundreds of holes through miles of gravel in the hot sun. Hell, with the gas-powered jackhammer in his toolbox, not even concrete would stop him.

His smart-ass co-workers called him the LUST—Leaky Underground Storage Tanks—man. Steadman couldn't imagine a less-suited acronym. He found nothing lusty about gasoline contaminating the groundwater. And he hadn't lusted for anybody or anything in a long, long time. He'd been given this nomadic grunt-work as punishment for his behavior on his last project at the civil engineering firm which specialized in hazardous waste cleanup. He'd been head geologist in the remediation of a large chemical plant. On his first day, he learned that for years the plant had been dumping blood red chemical by-products into the Alabama River. This was no surprise, but what pissed him off was that each morning two clueless black workers—without safety gear—had been sent out in a motorboat to net the dead fish floating on the surface. Steadman, before several laborers restrained him, had nearly shoved the plant engineer into the river.

He was three feet into his fourth hole, the dry dirt growing softer farther down, when the cellular phone in his truck chirped.

"Happy birthday to me," his father's dry voice sang, off-key.

After two choruses, Steadman interrupted him. "It's not your birthday yet."

"Hell, I know that, boy. It's tomorrow."

"Try December," Steadman said. "Five more months."

"Knock off the bullcrap and give me a hint, squirt."

Steadman sat on the tailgate, remembering that two days ago had been his mother's birthday; she'd been dead six years and this wasn't the first year he'd forgotten. "Dad," he said, "are you okay? Do the nurses know you're on the phone?"

"The hell with them, it's not *their* fiftieth."

It's not yours either, Steadman thought. His father was seventy-eight; this was his first year in the home.

"Bigger than a shoebox, I hope," his father said.

"What is?"

"My present. That goddamn dog you gave me last year must've run off."

The dog, a black Lab, a gift from Steadman's mother, had died of old age a decade ago. Steadman moved the phone to his other ear. He recalled that on trips into the country his father had always picked up hitchhikers, but made them ride in the back of the truck with the dog.

"Dad," Steadman said. "Listen. I've got one for you: crows."

"Easy. A murder."

This was a childhood road game; his father used to name an animal and Steadman was supposed to give its group title: an army of frogs, a parliament of owls, like that.

"Turtles," Steadman said.

"Let's see . . ." His father would do this all day, like a dog who never tired of fetching. "A bale."

"How about . . ." Steadman looked over by the gas pumps. "Rhinoceroses."

A pause, and Steadman pictured his father, who still wore the safety glasses required by his last job. He'd be standing at the pay phone, in his blue jumpsuit, right hand tapping his ample belly. Probably wearing his steel-toe work shoes, too.

"A pride?" he said. "Pride of rhinos?"

Behind Steadman a door slammed. Kilpatrick came limping around the building carrying his folding chair and a six-pack. He suddenly looked smaller.

Steadman stood up. "Dad, I'll call you later."

Kilpatrick opened the chair and sat in the narrow strip of shade the building offered and watched and drank as Steadman resumed digging, twisting the auger deeper into the ground. He thought he could smell gas already.

"Regular divining rod, ain't you?" Kilpatrick said, crossing his legs. He didn't have socks, which bothered Steadman. Like the smelly bastard was on vacation. "I do declare," he said, "you plumb determined to shut me down, ain't you?"

Steadman wiped sweat from his eyes. "You know what? If you want the truth, I'd rather not."

"The hell," Kilpatrick said. "You so goddamn eager to ruin a fellow's living you'll find some gas in the ground if you have to

pump it there your own damn self. That'll be my last sale," he
said to the sky, "three gallons for this here smart aleck to pour
in the dirt."

"You trot on over here," Steadman said. "Stick your snout in
this hole, see what you smell."

Kilpatrick stubbed out his half-smoked cigarette and put it
behind his ear. Steadman stepped aside and rubbed his biceps as
the old man came over and squatted, steadying himself on the
auger handle, which stood upright like a detonator. He made loud
sniffing sounds.

"What you smell there?" Steadman asked.

"Not a thing."

"How about that." Steadman stooped beside Kilpatrick. "I
declare if I don't smell gasoline."

"Shit," Kilpatrick said. He belched. "You smell what you want
to. If you was horny enough, you'd smell pussy in that hole."

"I don't guess you'd strike your lighter and hold it there,"
Steadman said, taking the old man's elbow to help him up.

Kilpatrick yanked his arm away.

"Got me a boy," he said. "Played ball for Auburn. If he was
here today, he'd knock your dick in the dirt and we'd let that
goddamn handle there be your grave marker." He stalked off,
stopping to collect his chair and beer.

The hole Steadman had been digging was four inches across
and three feet deep. The goods. That's what his father had called
the petroleum deposits he'd found. Steadman knelt and took a
handful of soil and let it fall through his fingers. He longed to
touch something undeveloped, uncontaminated. His father used
to come home excited about a pocket of crude they'd hit. He
would kiss Mom on the lips, then scoop her and Steadman into
his lap and tell them how the dinosaurs had died mysteriously,

how after millions of years, fermenting in the earth, they'd become oil. As he fell asleep those nights, Steadman imagined himself a famous archaeologist in a field jacket, a miner's light on his pith helmet, brush in hand, whisking away age-old dust to uncover the prehistoric bones of an unknown species, a rib cage the size of a ship's hull, a skull big enough to sleep in.

He got to his feet and went to the truck after soil sample jars. Soon he had them filled and neatly labeled. He brushed himself off, then got into the truck and pulled to the pumps to buy gas, if it hadn't all leaked out. The phone rang, his father again, with the right answer: *"A crash, goddammit. A crash of rhinos."* Steadman said he'd call him back later.

The unleaded pump was slower even than Kilpatrick: four cents . . . six cents . . . eight cents. . . . Steadman thought he'd be staring at the rhinoceros all day. He'd seen such things as a kid on tractor excursions when he and his father stopped for gas, each station as they drove deeper and deeper into the country stranger than the one before. In those days, owners often tried to attract customers with gimmicks—a two-headed pig preserved in a vat of alcohol, an albino rattlesnake that swallowed live opossums, free Choctaw arrowheads.

Kilpatrick's rhino, though, seemed more impressive: stretching past the regular gas pump on one end and the unleaded on the other, it was almost as long as Steadman's truck and nearly its breadth. With the pump running, he approached the rhino and touched its flank, gray and dry and rough as the side of a mountain. He brought his fingers to his nose; they smelled musty and leathery, a little oily, like an old saddle.

Clumps of stiff hair stuck out of the rhinoceros's leg joints and hung from its low-slung belly. Its eyes were marble, sad, bovine, and Steadman imagined it chewing grass in an African field, egrets and wrens across its broad shoulders and back. If any lion or water buffalo wandered too close, the rhino would toss its great tank of a head, horn slicing through the air like a scimitar. He slid his fingers down the slope of its neck and along the stiff ears, the bony eye ridges, the snout, the smaller lumplike horn and the larger, more formidable curved horn. Something rose in Steadman's chest and his fingertips tingled. It felt like he was touching his own past.

"My boy done that," Kilpatrick said. He stood in the office door with his hands in his pockets. "Got him a job in a carnival after he tore up his knee playing ball. That rhino died and him and some of his friends, clowns and midgets and shit, they tied it on a trailer and stole it before anybody could burn it or whatever the hell you'd do with a dead rhino." Kilpatrick chuckled. "That crazy boy skinned it and mounted it. He weren't too smart, but he was a swooft running back and hell on wheels in taxidermy."

Steadman pressed his shoulder against the rhinoceros's flank. He could barely move it. It had small, delicate legs and its feet, except for the one lifted, were nailed to wooden planks with inlets for a forklift.

"What does he weigh?" Steadman asked.

"She," the old man said, joining him. "Three, three-fifty, I reckon. My boy was a strong one. Lift half of anything."

Steadman whistled. A wolf spider had laced a web between the rhino's horns. He flicked the spider off and pulled away the web.

"Would you sell her?" he asked.

Kilpatrick snorted. "Reckon I'm fixing to have to sell everything." He wiped his lips with his black rag. "Well, they's folks'll pay a heap for that big horn by itself. Them poachers overseas say if you grind it up in a powder it's like giving a woman a bucket of goddamn oysters."

"What if," Steadman said, "I could let you keep your station?"
Kilpatrick regarded him.

"I could rig something . . ." Steadman said. "You've gotta have leak detection, that's all there is to it. If you don't, we'll both get caught. . . ."

He studied the ground at his feet, dirt he knew deep down was contaminated. You couldn't guess what might happen below the topsoil when you mixed things up. He'd worked one project where several tons of buried insecticide waste had been accidently discovered by a backhoe; the sludge had eaten through the metal barrels it had been stored in, and mixing with each other and the minerals in the soil, had formed a strange new chemical combination. The unlucky backhoe driver had died instantly from the murky green cloud that belched out of the ground.

Steadman walked into the road, hazy with heat as far as he could see. For a moment he thought a truck was coming, an eighteen-wheeler, but it was only a mirage. Shading his eyes, dizzy with heat, he barely heard the gas pump click off.

"Guess you were right the first time," he told Kilpatrick.

On the clean side of the station, where the tanks weren't buried, Steadman replaced the fake pipe he'd pulled out of the ground. He used a sledgehammer to drive it deep, then tamped the dirt tight with the handle. He resumed with the auger and began digging the first of four holes around the fake ports. In the widening strip of shade, Kilpatrick watched and drank beer and smoked and crossed and uncrossed his legs.

His shirt off, Steadman augered into the night. At about six feet down, groundwater started seeping into the holes—he saw it with his flashlight: clear, uncontaminated: the goods. He kept digging.

Kilpatrick rose once and limped toward him and handed him a beer. The old man turned and walked several feet away and took a leak while Steadman drank, then he came back for the empty bottle and returned to his chair. In the distance a coyote began to howl and Kilpatrick yelled "Shet up!" and the howling stopped.

Steadman finished digging just after nine-thirty, in the bright moonlight. A car had passed a few minutes earlier, and only now did he comprehend it. It had slowed, and a black face had peered out the open passenger window, and a black hand had waved. Had Steadman waved back?

At his truck, he slid four eight-foot-long PVC pipes from the side rack.

Kilpatrick, who'd been napping, woke and said, "What you up to now?"

"These are your monitoring wells," Steadman grunted, twisting a pipe into the first hole. "The way they work is, when I stick 'em in the ground, they fill up with water. If the water was contaminated, like it probably is on the other side, it'd have an oily sheen on top of it. But over here, you shine your flashlight in there you'll just see clean water. If the EPA comes to check on you, these ones'll be clear."

Steadman forced the last pipe in the ground until all but eight inches showed. "There," he said, screwing on its cap. "Tomorrow I'll come pour cement around here so nobody'll be inclined to check your authenticity."

Kilpatrick's Camel glowed. A strange sound came from the darkness, a fart maybe. Or a grunt of approval.

"One more thing," Steadman said, disassembling the auger. "Tomorrow that rhino comes with me."

"I'll vacuum her tonight," Kilpatrick said. "You can borry my trailer."

After a moment, the two men shook hands.

The next morning at the office, Steadman FedExed the jars of soil from his yard to the lab in Savannah. The results would be back in a week. He popped his head into the secretary's office and told her that Kilpatrick's Sinclair station had been a bust, that the old man already had leak detection. Then he told her it was his father's birthday; he was taking the day off. Ignoring her raised eyebrows, Steadman walked down the hall and went outside to his truck. With eight bags of quick-dry cement, he drove to Kilpatrick's.

The old man sat smoking in his office beside the open Coke machine. The unleaded gas pump still showed the eighteen dollars Steadman had bought yesterday. Kilpatrick jerked his thumb toward the back of the station.

The rhinoceros stood on the trailer, held tight by chains and come-alongs. Kilpatrick walked out from under the shed, hands in pockets. He directed Steadman in backing the truck to the trailer. The rhino's skin was clean, its eyes polished. Smelling of Lysol, it looked ready to stomp those feet, break loose from the puny chains and come-alongs, and charge.

"What you say," Kilpatrick said.

Steadman paused, a bag of cement on each shoulder. "Cooler today."

The old man squinted at the sky. "Yep. Might rain."

"Might."

Steadman poured cement around the wells, adding water from a leaky garden hose, while Kilpatrick hitched the trailer, a cigarette dangling from his black lips. Now and again he coughed. When he'd finished, Steadman walked to the trailer. Kilpatrick was wiring the taillights.

"How come your son gave you the rhino?" Steadman asked.

Kilpatrick didn't look up. "Don't remember," he said.

Together, they threw a tarp across the rhinoceros, then stepped back to inspect the job. It seemed illegal, transporting something so large, so threatening. But that worry was soon shrinking in Steadman's mirror as the truck kicked up dust enough to blot Kilpatrick from sight. A hell of a lot bigger than a shoebox, Steadman thought, picturing the rhino beside azaleas, surrounded by old people at the nursing home, his father among them, touching and stroking the dangerous beast with lust in their fingertips, a birthday gift ancient, faithful, unforgettable. Birds would collect on the rhino's back and Steadman knew his father would impress everyone by identifying them.

As he drove away from Kilpatrick's, Steadman pretended the rhino chased him, and like a child running at night, he went faster and faster. But the rhinoceros stayed close behind, its eyes tiny and clear, nose low, horn inches away from Steadman's gas tank.

instinct

Five years ago, Henry was driving home from the wastewater treatment plant when something caught his eye. He turned left off County 151 and pulled to the shoulder. For several minutes he sat, staring at the backs of his hands, which seemed as they clutched the steering wheel to belong to someone else. After a moment, the right hand put the gear lever into reverse.

It was a yard sale he'd passed, colorful junk spread on card tables under pecan trees. Two ten-speed bicycles leaned against a table beside a wooden knife rack, and a trampoline in the background had a sign that said MAKE OFFER. The woman conducting the sale wore a long skirt and an Alabama baseball cap and sat on a faded love seat. She closed the paperback she'd been reading when Henry stepped out of his truck. He wore his uniform pants from the plant and an undershirt.

The claw-footed bathtub was behind the tables. Coming the other way, he might never have seen it.

"Hot today," the woman said, without rising. She squinted and looked down the road and fanned herself with the book. The house behind her was red brick, two-story, dormer windows with drapes, not blinds, which Henry liked. A garden hose lay coiled next to the steps.

While she watched from the love seat, he walked to the bathtub and, looking into it, knelt in the wet grass. The porcelain was dirty, some rusty stains. But the drain plug was still there, attached by a tiny greenish chain. He ran his fingers along the tub's rim. He didn't like how the claw feet were sunk half an inch into the dirt.

"It's an antique," the woman said. She still hadn't gotten up. Henry thought she ought to be here with him, staring into the tub. As if remembering, he saw a woman's leg, a woman younger than this woman, her leg raised, soaped, over the rim.

"Belonged to my grandmother," the saleswoman went on. "She passed two years ago."

"How much?" Henry asked, and she finally stood.

He paid without haggling.

In his truck, he took the tub to his uncle L.J.'s hunting cabin in the middle of the two hundred acres of scrubby pine woods and wrestled it down into the root cellar, dragged it beside the butcher's block where the old man had cleaned the deer and wild pigs he'd killed. To hook up the tub, Henry could branch a T-pipe from the industrial sink in the corner, which his uncle had gotten at a hospital auction and which had pedals so you could turn the water on and off with your foot.

Uncle L.J. had died several years before, emphysema and a brain tumor the size of a golf ball. Henry's mother kept saying they ought to sell that old falling-down place with its deer heads and the stuffed bobcat and turkey beards, ought to sell the useless dead land, too, but Henry knew that in his thirty-eight years, they'd never gotten rid of anything.

Two years later he woke on a Sunday morning. His mother was calling him, saying he'd be late for church. He went to the door and peeped out. She stood by the hall stand, putting on lipstick.

"I'm staying home," he called. "Don't feel good."

She closed her purse. "You were out late again last night," she said. "Drinking, I expect. It's no wonder you're ill. John?"

His father appeared, in a tie but no jacket. "Come on down, Henry the Great."

"No." Henry closed the door and locked it. He imagined the old man jingling the keys in his pocket and scratching his bald spot. His mother catching his father's eye in the mirror.

But soon the front door closed. At the window by his bed, he parted the drapes and watched them climb gravely into the car, his mother in her yellow church hat. They sat for a moment and he realized they were praying. For him, he knew. Then the Chrysler's brake lights blinked and the car moved down the drive.

In the attic, he rolled the soft extra mattress into a ball and tied it with a piece of nylon rope. He pushed it across the dusty floor and out the trapdoor, nearly toppling an end table with a vase of daisies on it. The mattress came down the stairs easily, and out the front door. Driving to his uncle's cabin, which was nearly ready, he began to shiver in the heat.

A year ago a school bus stopped at the treatment plant. Henry looked up from adjusting an aerator pump with a pipe wrench. He took off his gloves. The bus door opened and the driver stepped out; behind him the seats were empty of children and he stood before Henry and pointed across the plant yard to the water storage pond.

"What're them balloons you got floating there?" he asked. "Scientific devices?"

Henry squinted at the pond and told the driver no, they were rubbers.

"Rubbers?"

"Condoms," Henry said, and explained that how after people had sex the man often tied a knot in the rubber and flushed it down the toilet. In the sewer system it gets hot, Henry went on. Gases in the rubber build up and expand and when the rubbers come out of the sewer into the treatment pond they float like balloons.

"I believe that one over there's a French tickler," Henry said, pointing with the wrench.

"Christ," the bus driver said. "What'll I tell the kids? They changed our route and now the children keep asking me what them balloons are."

"Tell 'em they're titties," Henry said.

"Titties," the driver said, chuckling.

Later, in moonlight, Henry brought his pellet rifle to the plant and sat on the dock with a package of cigarettes and shot the rubbers, one by one.

This evening Henry slips out of his parents' house. His mother and father are snoozing beside the fireplace, the TV on. It's about thirty-five degrees out, but getting colder. The radio says snow is possible. Driving, he finds himself humming. He goes to the Key West for a Jack and Coke. The place is dead. He and the bartender talk about snow. The bartender says he's from Maryland and it snows there a heap. Henry says sure it does. The bartender says he used to work nights in a hospital in D.C. and, no matter how hard it snowed, you had to be at work for your shift. You couldn't miss, you had to be prepared. He says they're ready for snow there. Plows all over the place. Down here, he says, you get a spoonful of snow once in five years and they shut down the fucking city.

Outside, Henry hurries to his truck. He glances at the night sky past the streetlights. When he looks back down, a woman is squatting beside his tire. He watches her, thinking she's peeing in the street, but she picks something up, a piece of electrical wire.

"Hello," he says.

She jumps, then, seeing his face, laughs. "You scared the shit outta me."

"You okay?" he asks.

"You a cop?"

He shakes his head.

"Then I'm Brenda," she says. "You want a date?"

Across the street is an alley with a Dumpster in the back. This is downtown and nothing moves. A mist is in the air now, it stings his cheeks. She moves closer to him, urgently, shivering with cold. She has blond hair that needs washing and she is very thin.

"I want to show you something," she says. "Think of it as an advertisement." When she reaches into her purse Henry imagines she might pull out a badge and arrest him for soliciting prostitution. He has a record already, for trying to set his high school gym on fire years ago. But she brings Polaroid pictures out of her purse. He has to squint to see them but knows they're shots of her nude. There's one where she lies on her stomach on a bed. You can see her bottom and part of one breast, though no nipple. The next shows her pubic hair, and both breasts. Then one with her sitting astride an exercise bike. And one with her in a bathtub.

"Can I buy these?" he asks.

"Depends," Brenda says. She stares at him for a long time, so long he doesn't like it. "Look," she says. "I'm in kind of a bad way. What's your name?"

"Donald," Henry says.

"Okay, Donny, look. Give me twenty bucks and a ride, and I'll blow you. Deal?"

He looks at the pictures again. "Them," he says.

She snatches them away. "Christ, Donny. It's cold. Look how you're shivering."

She has long red fingernails that are chipped, and he thinks her hair might be a wig.

"Okay, thirty," she says. "For the pictures and nothing else. You pay first."

In the truck, she switches the heater on high. She changes the radio from country to rap. She turns it up. "Got a cigarette?"

He hands her his pack and lighter. She lights one. "So what-all drugs've you done?"

He says not many. The truth is none.

"Turn here," she says, pointing a long nail. He obeys. "Tell me something, Donny-boy—" She's going through her purse. "Why do you hate women? I'm not judging you," she says. "All my rides do. I'm just curious. Was it your mother? Some ex-girlfriend? Who?"

He shrugs, wonders what to say, but she brings something out of her purse. She holds it against the dash lights.

"You ever seen that?" she asks.

A dirty-white crystal, the size of an aspirin.

"Crack," Henry says.

"You guessed it, Donny. Got a knife?"

He says he doesn't, though he does, in his pocket, a birthday present from his parents several years ago. He thinks of them now. They'll be done with supper, his mother in the kitchen putting dishes away. Wiping the counter. His father in the den, watching the Alabama Tide on TV. They'll be asking each other where Henry has gotten off to.

"No prob," Brenda says. "Nobody can improvise like an addict. Turn here, Donny."

She takes the piece of electrical wire and lights a match and holds the match to the wire. She doesn't see that Henry passes the turn. It will be a while before she realizes. When the plastic coating on the wire begins to melt, she strips it off. She takes a pen from her purse and pulls the ink cartridge out. She forces the wire into the barrel of the pen. Then, holding the wire in place with her long nails, she breaks off a corner of the crack and pushes it into the opposite end of the pen. She taps the rock gently with a nail. Strikes another match.

She lights the pipe and inhales, using the wire for a filter. Outside, rain has begun to fall and there are pine trees. Inside, her eyes have become red and dreamy and the truck has filled with smoke.

"Do you want to die?" Henry asks.

"Spare the sermon," she says, offering him the pipe.

He takes it, rolls down his window and without thinking throws it out.

"Hey," Brenda says.

Tomorrow, when Henry comes back through, he will have to find the pipe. He makes note of a pine stump and a large hole in the road. Brenda is yelling now, but he barely hears. He is already living in tomorrow, already on his knees in the stiff cold grass, finding the pipe, which will be frozen and will snap easily in his fingers.

alaska

Our aim was this: Alaska.

To abandon Mobile at dawn without telling anybody, not even our girlfriends or our boss at the plant. Bruce knew a bail jumper who got a deckhand job on a crab boat off the Alaskan coast where she made five hundred dollars a day. Bruce was divorced for the third time and I'd never been married, so we planned to sell our cars and Bruce's house trailer and buy an olive drab Ford four-wheel-drive pickup with a camper, fill it full of those sharp green pinecones hard as hand grenades. Bruce'd heard you could sell those suckers for five bucks apiece in New England.

They're crazy up there, he said.

Driving through Georgia and Tennessee, we'd look for tent revivals where they had faith healing. If we found a good one we'd stop and visit a service. Bruce would fake heart disease and I'd be an alcoholic—to make it convincing, he said, I'd have to belch and stumble and splash on rum like aftershave. He would grimace, moan, and clutch his left arm, until we had the whole congregation praying for us. When the ushers passed the KFC buckets for donations, we'd shrug and say we were flat broke, just poor travelers. Homeless.

Bruce had stolen his second ex-wife's Polaroid camera, which we'd keep handy for making pictures—hawks on fenceposts, grizzly bears, church marquees that said THE LORD IS COMING SOON,

125

then right under that BINGO 8:00 EVERY TUESDAY. We'd have a stack of books-on-tape from the public library, too: John Grisham, Stephen King and even self-help. In the Badlands of South Dakota, when we pulled off the road to sleep in the back of the truck with our feet sticking out, we'd play an *Improve Your Vocabulary* tape, learn words like *eclectic* and *satyr*.

At night we'd stop in dives, me in my dark glasses and Bruce in his eelskin cowboy boots. There'd be smoky harems of women interested in such eclectic guys, and they'd insist on buying us boilermakers. When I picked up a babe, I'd take the truck and leave Bruce arm-wrestling a drunk welder at the bar. Or if he got lucky and split with a startling honey, I'd amble to the jukebox and punch up John Prine and lure my dream girl away from the line-dancing bikers and cowboys. In the middle of the fight, I'd crawl bleeding out the back and sleep on a rock next to a cow skull and wait until the olive drab truck topped the hill in the morning.

We'd make pictures of the girls, too. You'd be surprised how many get off from posing in motel rooms, Bruce said. He would "let on" to some of the drunker ladies that we were advance photographers for the swimsuit issue, our names Abe Z. and Horatio. At the other end of the bar I'd be telling them that we were scientists from Texas researching barn owls. But to that adventurous woman running the pool table, the redhead wearing tight cutoff jeans, the kind of woman you know has a green iguana tattooed on her hip, to her we'd tell the truth: Alaska. Bruce said she could tag along, but he was sure she'd get homesick thousands of miles before the crab boat. Imagine the scene: some dusty Wyoming ghost town and this woman sobbing and hugging our necks, angry that she's such a crybaby. She would climb the steps and we'd watch her sad pretty face in the window as the bus lurched off, and when she was gone Bruce would sigh with relief and, after a few drinks, we'd get in the truck and go north.

I'd miss her terribly.

If we saw the right brand of dog—it was a mutt we wanted, the ugliest in the lower forty-eight—we'd stop and bribe him with fast food. He could sit between us on the seat and lick our hands, and if he farted we could look at each other and yell, "Was that you?" and crank the windows down furiously. And, of course, we'd pick up chicks hitchhiking. When we got one, she could sit between us and hold the dog (we'd name him Handsome) and croon to him. We'd go days out of our way to get her home, but we wouldn't be crass and say, "Ass, gas or grass." All our rides would be free.

Because manners *were* important, we thought. So eating in truck stops, we'd put our napkins in our laps and remove our caps and say "Yes, ma'am" to the flirting women at nearby tables, even the Yankees, who wouldn't be used to such gentlemen. We would smile and wink and gather our doggie bags and leave 50 percent tips. Our waitresses would long to follow us, and the pretty gas station checkout girls would lean over their cash registers to read our names off the backs of our belts—not only because of our unusual looks and ugly dog, but our cultured southern manners.

And sportsmen to the end, we'd skid off the road when we saw a private golf course. We'd step out of the trees in our loud pants and vault the fence and drive our used balls into the clouds, needing binoculars to watch the hole-in-ones three hundred yards away. The serious golfers, in their berets, would frown at each other as we played through, carrying only one driver each, and when the stern club attendant came, we'd disappear into the woods like satyrs and reappear magically at the clubhouse bar.

Or we'd stop if we found a good secluded pond, rig our rods with Snagless Sallys and pork rinds, cast into the hard-to-reach, around cypress knees, into grasses, keeping our lines flexible as the largemouth bass tore through the murk with the rind whipping against its gills. We'd set the hooks like pros and play the fish perfectly, then grill the shining wet lunkers over a campfire that night and sip the moonshine we'd stolen from bootleggers in Virginia. Handsome would prowl the pond and court his first she-wolf, the two of them baying softly, and in the firelight Bruce would uncase his mandolin and I'd warm up my harmonica, and we'd play tender ballads, love songs, so sweet the woods would grow still and sad around us, and just before we'd begin to lament all the people and places we'd left behind, things we'd never see again, we would stop playing as if on cue and look at each other, suddenly happy, remembering Alaska, waiting for us.

poachers

At dawn on the first day of April, the three Gates brothers banked their ten-foot aluminum boat in a narrow slough of dark water. They tied their hounds, strapped on their rifles and stepped out, ducking black magnolia branches heavy with rain and Spanish moss. The two thin younger brothers, denim overalls tucked into their boots, lugged between them a Styrofoam cooler of iced fish, coons and possums. The oldest brother—twenty, bearded, heavy-set—carried a Sunbeam Bread sack of eels in his coat pocket. Hooked over his left shoulder was the pink body of a fawn they'd shot and skinned, and, over the right, a stray dog to which they'd done the same. With the skins and heads gone and the dog's tail chopped off, they were difficult to tell apart.

The Gateses climbed the hill, clinging to vines and saplings, slipping in the red clay, their boots coated and enormous by the time they stepped out of the woods. For a moment they stood in the road, looking at the gray sky, the clouds piling up. The two younger ones, Neil and Dan, set the cooler down. Kent, the oldest, removed his limp cap and squeezed the water from it. His brothers did the same. Then Kent nodded and they picked up the cooler. They rounded a curve and crossed a one-lane bridge, stopping to piss over the rail into creek water high from all the rain, then went on, passing houses on either side: dark warped boards with knotholes big enough to look through and cement

129

blocks for steps. Black men appeared in doors and windows to watch them go by—to most of these people they were something not seen often, something nocturnal and dangerous. Along this stretch of the Alabama River, everyone knew that the brothers' father, Boo Gates, had married a girl named Anna when he was thirty and she was seventeen, and that the boys had been born in quick succession, with less than a year between them.

But few outside the family knew that a fourth child—a daughter, unnamed—had been stillborn, and that Boo had buried her in an unmarked grave in a clearing in the woods behind their house. Anna died the next day and the three boys, dirty and naked, watched their father's stoop-shouldered descent into the earth as he dug her grave. By the time he'd finished it was dark and the moon had come up out of the trees and the boys lay asleep upon each other in the dirt like wolf pups.

The name of this community, if it could be called that, was Lower Peach Tree, though as far as anybody knew there'd never been an Upper Peach Tree. Scattered along the leafy banks of the river were ragged houses, leaning and drafty, many empty, caving in, so close to the water they'd been built on stilts. Each April floods came and the crumbling land along the bank would disappear, and each May, when the flood waters receded, a house or two would be gone.

Upriver, near the lock and dam, stood an old store, a slanting, weathered building with a steep tin roof and a stovepipe in the back. Two rusty gas pumps on the left, beside the road. The regular pump, empty for years, had a garbage bag tied over it. Around the store the mimosa trees sagged, waterlogged. In front, long steps led up to the door, where in the window a red sign said OPEN. Inside to the right, like a bar, a polished maple counter ran along the wall. Behind the counter hung a rack with wire pegs for tools, hardware and fishing tackle. To the left were rows of shelves made of boards and concrete blocks, and beyond the shelves a Coca-Cola cooler buzzed faintly by the wall.

The store owner, an old man named Kirxy, had bad knees, and this weather settled around his joints like rot. For most of his life he'd been married and lived in a nice two-story house on highway 35, fireplaces in every bedroom, a china cabinet. But when his wife died two years ago, cancer, he found it easier to avoid the house, to keep the bills paid and the grass mowed but the doors locked, to spend nights in the store, to sleep in the back room on the army cot and to warm his meals of corned beef and beef stew on a hot plate. He didn't mind that people had all but stopped coming to the store. As long as he served a few longstanding customers, he thought he'd stick around. He had his radio and the Thomasville station and money enough. He liked the area and knew his regulars weren't the kind to drive half an hour to the nearest town. For those few people, Kirxy would go once a week to Grove Hill to shop for goods he'd resell, marking up the price just enough for a reasonable profit. He didn't need the money; it was just good business.

Liquor-wise, the county was dry, but that didn't stop Kirxy. For his regulars, he would serve plastic cups of the cheap whisky he bought in the next county or bottles of beer he kept padlocked in the old refrigerator in back. For these regulars, he would break packages of cigarettes and keep them in a cigar box and sell them for a dime apiece, a nickel stale. Aspirins were seven cents each. He would open boxes of shotgun shells or cartridges and sell them for amounts that varied according to caliber, and he'd been known to find specialty items—paperback novels, explosives and, once, an old magneto telephone.

At Euphrates Morrisette's place, Kent Gates pounded on the back door. In Morrisette's yard a cord of wood was stacked between two fenceposts and covered by a green tarp, brick halves holding the tarp down. A tire swing, turning slowly and full of rainwater, hung from a pine limb. When Morrisette appeared—he was a large, bald black man—Kent pointed to the fawn and dog hanging on the porch rail. Morrisette put on reading glasses and squinted at both. "How 'bout that," he said, stroking his chin. "Be right out, young mens." He closed the door. Kent sat on the porch edge and his brothers on the steps. A skinny wet dog trotted from under the house, wagging its tail, and Dan began to pet it. When he found a swollen blue tick in its ear, he pulled it off and flicked it across the yard.

The door opened and Morrisette came out with three pint jars of homemade whisky. Each brother took a jar and unscrewed its lid, sniffed the clear liquid. Morrisette set his steaming coffee cup on the windowsill. He fastened his suspenders, looking at the carcasses hanging over the rail. The brothers were already drinking, Dan still petting the dog, which had its head in his lap.

"Where's that girl?" Kent asked, his face twisted from the sour whisky.

"My stepdaughter, you mean?" Morrisette's Adam's apple pumped in his throat. "She inside."

Far away a rooster crowed.

"Get her out here," Kent said. He drank again, shuddered.

"She ain't but fifteen."

Kent scratched his beard. "Just gonna look at her."

When they left, the stepdaughter was standing on the porch in her white nightgown, barefoot and rubbing the sleep from her eyes. The brothers backed away clanking with hardware and blushing and grinning at her, Morrisette's jaw clenched. The dog watched them go, then turned and trotted back underneath the house.

Sipping from their jars, they took the bag of eels down the road to the half-blind conjure woman who stood waiting on her porch. Her house, with its dark drapes and empty birdcages dangling from the eaves, seemed to be slipping off into the gully. The younger brothers wiped their noses on their sleeves and shifted from foot to foot by the gate as Kent walked across the muddy yard and held the bag out. She snatched the eels from him, squinting into the bag with her good eye. Grunting, she paid them from a dusty cloth sack on her apron and muttered to herself as Kent turned and walked through her gate and the three of them went up the dirt road. Only Dan, the youngest, looked back.

They peddled the rest of the things from their cooler, then left through the dump, pausing while Kent and Neil shot at liquor bottles Dan threw into the air. Out of ammunition, they stumbled down the ravine in the rain, following the water's edge to their boat. In the back, Kent wedged his jar between his thighs and ran the trolling motor with his foot. His brothers leaned against the walls of the boat, facing opposite banks, no sound but rain and the low hum of the motor. They drank silently, holding the burning whisky in the hollows of their cheeks before gathering the will to swallow. Along the banks, fallen trees held thick strands of cottonmouth, black sparkling creatures dazed and slow from winter, barely able to move. If not for all the rain, they might still be hibernating, comatose in the banks of the river or beneath the soft yellow underbellies of rotten logs.

Rounding a bend, the brothers saw a small boat downriver, its engine clear, loud and unfamiliar. Heading this way. The man in the boat lifted a hand in greeting. He wore a green poncho and a dark hat covered with plastic. Kent shifted his foot, turning the trolling motor, and steered them toward the bank, giving the stranger a wide berth. He felt for their outboard's crank rope while Neil and Dan faced forward and sat on the boat seats. The man drawing closer didn't look much older than Kent. He cut his engine and coasted up beside them, smiling.

"Morning, fellows," he said, showing a badge. "New district game warden."

The brothers looked straight ahead, as if he weren't there. The warden's engine was steaming, a flock of geese passed overhead. Dan slipped his hands inside the soft leather collars of two dogs, who'd begun to growl.

"You fellows oughta know," the warden said, pointing his long chin to the rifle at Neil's feet, "that it's illegal to have those guns loaded on the river. I'm gonna have to check 'em. I'll need to see some licenses, too."

When he stood, the dogs jumped forward, toenails scraping aluminum. Dan jerked them back and glanced at Kent.

Kent spat into the brown water. He met the warden's eyes, and in an instant knew the man had seen the telephone rig in the floor of their boat.

"Pull to the bank!" the warden yelled, drawing a pistol. "Y'all are under arrest for poaching!"

The Gateses didn't move. One of the dogs began to claw the hull and the others joined him. A howl rose.

"Shut 'em up!" The warden's face had grown blotchy and red.

The spotted hound broke free and sprang over the gunnel, slobber strung from its teeth, and the man most surprised by the game warden's shot seemed to be the game warden himself. His face drained of color as the noise echoed off the water and died in the bent black limbs and the cattails that bobbed in the current. The bullet had passed through the front dog's neck and smacked into the bank behind them, missing Dan by inches. The dog collapsed, and there was an instant of silence before the others, now loose, clattered overboard into the water, red-eyed, tangled in their leashes, trying to swim.

"Pull to the goddamn bank!" the warden yelled. "Right now!"

Scowling, Kent leaned and spat. He moved his thirty-thirty aside. Using the shoulders of his brothers for balance, he made his way to the prow. Neil, his cheekbones flecked with dog blood, moved to the back to keep the boat level. At the front, Kent reached into the water and took the first dog by its collar, lifted the kicking form and set it streaming and shivering behind him. His brothers turned their faces away as it shook off the water.

Kent grabbed the rope that led to the big three-legged hound and pulled it in hand over hand until he could work his fingers under its collar. He gave Dan a sidelong look and together they hauled it in. Then Kent grabbed for the smaller bitch while Dan got the black-and-tan.

The warden watched them, his hips swaying with the rise and fall of the current. Rain was coming harder now, spattering against the boats.

Kneeling among the dogs, Kent unsnapped the leash and tossed the spotted hound overboard. It sank, then resurfaced and floated on its side, trailing blood. Kent's lower lip twitched. He looked at Neil and opened his mouth. Dan whispered to the dogs and placed his hands on two of their heads to calm them—they were retching and trembling and rolling their eyes fearfully at the trees.

Neil stood up with his hands raised, as if to surrender. When the game warden looked at him, relief softening his eyes, Kent jumped from his crouch into the other boat, his big fingers closing around the man's neck.

Later that morning, Kirxy had just unlocked the door and hung out the open sign when he heard the familiar rattle of the Gates truck. He sipped his coffee and limped behind the counter, sat on his stool. The boys came several times a week, usually in the afternoon, before they started their evenings of hunting and fishing. Kirxy would give them what supplies they needed—bullets, fishing line, socks, a new cap to replace one lost in the river. They would fill their truck and cans with gas. Eighteen-year-old Dan would get the car battery from the charger near the woodburning stove and replace it with the drained one from their boat's trolling motor. Kirxy would serve them coffee or Cokes—never liquor, not to boys—and they'd eat whatever they chose from the shelves, usually candy bars or barbecue potato chips, ignoring Kirxy's advice to eat healthier, Vienna sausages, Dinty Moore or Chef Boyardee.

Today they came in looking a little spooked, Kirxy thought. Neil stayed near the door, peering out, the glass fogging by his mouth. His arms folded. Dan went to the candy aisle and pocketed several Hershey bars. He left a trail of muddy boot prints behind him. Kirxy would have to mop later.

"Morning, young fellows," he said. "Coffee?"

Dan nodded. Kirxy filled a Styrofoam cup, then grinned as the boy loaded it with sugar.

"You take coffee with your sweetener?" he asked.

Kent leaned on the counter, inspecting the items hanging on their pegs, a hacksaw, a Lucky 13 lure, a set of Allen wrenches. A gizmo with several uses, knife, measuring tape, awl. He took off his cap and balled it in his fist. Kirxy could smell the booze on him.

"Y'all need something particular?" he asked.

"That spotted one you give us?" Kent said, not meeting his eyes. "Won't bark no more."

"She won't bark no more?"

"Naw. Tree 'em fine, but won't bark nary a time. Gotta shoot her."

His mouth full of chocolate, Dan looked at Kirxy. By the door, Neil unfolded his arms.

"No," Kirxy said. "Ain't no need for that, Kent. Do what that conjure woman recommends. Go out in the woods, find you a locust shell stuck to a tree. This is the time of year for 'em, if I'm not mistaken."

"Locust shell?" Kent asked.

"Yeah. Bring it back home and crunch it up in the dog's scraps, and that'll make her bark like she ought to."

Kent nodded to Kirxy and walked to the door. He went out, his brothers following.

"See you," Kirxy called. "You're welcome."

Dan waved with a Hershey bar and closed the door.

Kirxy stared after them for a time. It had been more than a year since they'd paid him anything, but he couldn't bring himself to ask for money; he'd even stopped writing down what they owed.

He got his coffee and limped from behind the counter to the easy chair by the stove. He shook his head at the muddy footprints on the candy aisle. He sat slowly, tucked a blanket around his legs, took out his bottle and added a splash to his coffee. Sipping, he picked up a novel—Louis L'Amour, *Sackett's Land*—and reached in his apron pocket for his glasses.

Though she had been once, the woman named Esther wasn't much of a regular in Kirxy's store these days. She lived two miles upriver in a shambling white house with massive magnolia trees in the yard. The house had a wraparound porch, and when it flooded you could fish from the back, sitting in the tall white rocking chairs, though you weren't likely to catch anything, a baby alligator maybe, or sometimes bullfrogs. Owls nested in the trees along her part of the river, but in this weather they'd grown quiet; she missed their hollow calling.

Esther was fifty. She'd had two husbands and six children who were gone and had ill feelings toward her. She'd had her female parts removed in an operation she was still paying for. Now she lived alone and, most of the time, drank alone. If the Gates boys hadn't passed out in their truck somewhere in the woods, they might stop by after a night's work. Esther would make them strong coffee and feed them salty fried eggs and link sausages, and some mornings, like today, she would get a faraway look in her eyes and take Kent's shirt collar in her fingers and lead him upstairs and watch him close the bathroom door and listen to the sounds of his bathing.

She smiled, knowing these were the only baths he ever took.

When he emerged, his long hair stringy, his chest flat and hard, she led him down the hall past the telephone nook to her bedroom. He crawled under the covers and watched her take off her gown and step out of her underwear. Bending, she looked in the mirror to fluff her hair, then climbed in beside him. He was gentle at first, curious, then rougher, the way she liked him to be. She closed her eyes, the bed frame rattling and bumping, her father's old pocket watch slipping off the nightstand. Water gurgled in the pipework in the walls as Neil took a bath, too, hoping for a turn of his own, which had never happened. At least not yet.

"Slow, baby," Esther whispered in Kent's ear. "It's plenty of time. . . ."

On April third it was still raining. Kirxy put aside his crossword to answer the telephone.

"Can you come on down to the lock and dam?" Goodloe asked. "We got us a situation developing here."

Kirxy disliked smart-ass Goodloe, but something in the sheriff's voice told him it was serious. On the news, he'd heard that the new game warden had been missing for two days. The authorities had dragged the river all night and had a helicopter in the air. Kirxy sat forward in his chair, waiting for his back to loosen a bit. He added a shot of whisky to his coffee and gulped it down as he shrugged into his denim jacket, zipping it up to his neck because he stayed cold when it rained. He put cotton balls in his ears and set his cap on his bald head, took his walking cane from beside the door.

In his truck, the four-wheel-drive engaged and the defroster on high, he sank and rose in the deep ruts, gobs of mud flying past his windows, the wipers swishing across his view. The radio announcer said it was sixty degrees, more rain on the way, then Loretta Lynn began to sing.

A mile from the lock and dam Kirxy passed the Grove Hill ambulance, axle-deep in mud. A burly black paramedic was wedging a piece of two-by-four beneath one of the rear tires while the bored-looking driver sat behind the wheel, smoking and racing the engine.

Kirxy slowed and rolled down his window. "Y'all going after a live one or a dead one?"

"Dead, Mr. Kirxy," the black man answered.

Kirxy nodded and accelerated. At the lock and dam, he could see a crowd of people and umbrellas and beyond them he saw the dead man, lying on the ground under a black raincoat. Some onlooker had begun to direct traffic. Goodloe and three deputies in yellow slickers stood near the body with their hands in their pockets.

Kirxy climbed out and people nodded somberly and parted to let him through. Goodloe, who'd been talking to his deputies, ceased as Kirxy approached and they stood looking at the raincoat.

"Morning, Sugarbaby," Kirxy said, using the nickname Goodloe hated. "Is this who I think it is?"

"Yep," Goodloe said. "Rookie game warden of the year."

With his cane, Kirxy pulled back the raincoat to reveal the white face. "Young fellow," he said.

There was a puddle beneath the dead man, twigs in his hair and a clove of moss in his breast pocket. With the rubber tip of his cane, Kirxy brushed a snail from the man's forehead. He bent and looked into the warden's left eye, which was partly open. He noticed the throat, the dark bruises there.

Goodloe unfolded a handkerchief and blew his nose, then wiped it. "Don't go abusing the evidence, Kirxy." He stuffed the handkerchief into his back pocket.

"Evidence? Now, Sugarbaby."

Goodloe exhaled and looked at the sky. "Don't shit me, Kirxy. You know good and well who done this. I expect they figure the law don't apply up here on this part of the river, the way things is been all these years. Them other wardens scared of 'em or feeling sorry for 'em. But I reckon that's fixing to change." He paused. "I had to place me a call to the capitol this morning. To let 'em know we was all outta game wardens. And you won't believe who they patched me through to."

Kirxy adjusted the cotton in his right ear.

"Old Frank David himself," the sheriff said. "Ain't nothing ticks him off more than this kind of thing."

A dread stirred in Kirxy's belly. "Frank David. Was he a relation of this fellow?"

"Teacher," Goodloe said. "Said he's been giving lessons to young game wardens over at the forestry service. He asked me a whole bunch of questions. Regular interrogation. Said this here young fellow was the cream of the crop. Best new game warden there was."

"Wouldn't know it from this angle," Kirxy said.

Goodloe grunted.

A photographer from the paper was studying the corpse. He glanced at the sky as if gauging the light. When he snapped the first picture, Kirxy was in it, like a sportsman.

"What'd you want from me?" he asked Goodloe.

"You tell them boys I need to ask 'em some questions, and I ain't fixing to traipse all over the county. I'll drop by the store this evening."

"If they're there, they're there," Kirxy said. "I ain't their damn father."

Goodloe followed him to the truck. "You might think of getting 'em a lawyer," he said through the window.

Kirxy started the engine. "Shit, Sugarbaby. Them boys don't
need a lawyer. They just need to stay in the woods, where they
belong. Folks oughta know to let 'em alone by now."

Goodloe stepped back from the truck. He smacked his lips. "I
don't reckon anybody got around to telling that to the deceased."

Driving, Kirxy remembered the Gates brothers when they were
younger, before their father shot himself. He pictured the three
blond heads in the front of Boo's boat as he motored upriver past
the store, lifting a solemn hand to Kirxy where he stood with a
broom on his little back porch. After Boo's wife and newborn
daughter had died, he'd taught those boys all he knew about the
woods, about fishing, tracking, hunting, killing. He kept them in
his boat all night as he telephoned catfish and checked his trotlines
and jugs and shot things on the bank. He'd given each of his sons
a job to do, one cranking the phone, another netting the stunned
catfish, the third adjusting the chain that dragged along the bottom and the wire which conducted electricity from the telephone's magnets into the water. Boo would tie a piece of rope
around his sons' waists and loop the other end to his own ankle
in case one of the boys fell overboard.

Downriver, in the moonlight, Kent would pull in the trotlines
while Dan handed him a cricket or catalpa worm for the hook.
Neil took the bass, perch or catfish Kent gave him and slit its soft
cold belly with a knife and ran two fingers up into the fish and
drew out its palmful of guts and dumped them overboard. Sometimes on warm nights grinnel or cottonmouths or young alligators

would follow them, drawn by blood. A danger, too, was catching a snake or snapping turtle on the trotline, and each night Boo whispered for Kent to be careful, to lift the line with a stick and see what he had there instead of using his bare hand.

During the morning they would leave the boat tied and the boys would follow their father's back through the trees from trap to trap, stepping when he stepped, not talking. Boo emptied the traps and rebaited them while behind him Kent put the carcasses in his squirrel pouch. In the afternoons, they gutted and skinned what they'd brought home. What time was left before dark they spent sleeping in the featherbed in the cabin where, barely a memory, their mother and sister had died.

After Boo's suicide, Kirxy had tried to look after the boys, their ages twelve, thirteen and fourteen—just old enough, Boo must've thought, to raise themselves. For a while Kirxy let them stay with him and his wife, who'd never had a child. He tried to send them to school, but they were past learning to read and write and got expelled the first day for fighting, ganging up on a black kid. They were past the kind of life Kirxy's wife was used to living. They scared her, the way they watched her with eyes narrowed into black lines, the way they ate with their hands, the way they wouldn't talk. What she didn't know was that from those years of wordless nights on the river and silent days in the woods they had developed a kind of language of their own, a language of the eyes, of the fingers, of the way a shoulder twitched, a nod of the head.

Because his wife's health wasn't good in those days, Kirxy had returned the boys to their cabin in the woods. He spent most Saturdays with them, trying to take up where Boo had left off, bringing them food and milk, clothes and new shoes, reading them books, teaching them things and telling stories. He'd worked out a deal with Esther, who used to take hot food to them in the evenings and wash their clothes. . . .

Slowing to let two buzzards hop away from a dead deer, Kirxy lit a cigarette and wiped the foggy windshield with the back of his hand. He thought of Frank David, Alabama's legendary game warden. There were dozens of stories about the man—Kirxy had heard and told them for years, had repeated them to the Gates boys, even made some up to try to scare them into obeying the law. Now the truth and the fictions were confused in his mind. He remembered one: A dark, moonless night, and two poachers use a spotlight to freeze a buck in the darkness and shoot it. They take hold of its wide rack of antlers and struggle to drag the big deer when suddenly they realize that now three men are pulling. The first poacher jumps and says, "Hey, it ain't supposed to be but two of us dragging this deer!"

And Frank David says, "Ain't supposed to be none of y'all dragging it."

The Gates boys came in the store just before closing, smelling like the river. Nodding to Kirxy, they went to the shelves and began selecting cans of things to eat. Kirxy poured himself a generous shot of whisky. He'd stopped by their cabin earlier and, not finding them there, left a quarter on the steps. A signal he hadn't used in years.

"Sheriff Goodloe's coming by tonight," he said to Kent. "Wants to ask if y'all know anything about that dead game warden."

Kent shot the other boys a look.

"Now I don't know if y'all've ever even seen that fellow," Kirxy

said, "and I'm not asking you to tell me." He paused, in case
they wanted to. "But that's what old Sugarbaby's gonna have on
his mind. If I was y'all, I just wouldn't tell him anything. Just say
I was at home, that I don't know nothing about any dead game
warden. Nothing at all."

Kent shrugged and walked down the aisle he was on and stared
out the back window, though there wasn't anything to see except
the trees, ghostly and bent, when lightning came. His brothers
took seats by the stove and began to eat. Kirxy watched, remembering when he used to read to them, *Tarzan of the Apes* and *The
Return of Tarzan*. The boys had wanted to hear the books over
and over—they loved the jungle, the elephants, rhinos, gorillas,
the anacondas thirty feet long. They would listen intently, their
eyes bright in the light of the stove, Dan holding in his small
dirty fingers the Slinky Kirxy had given him as a Christmas present, his lips moving along with Kirxy's voice, mouthing some of
the words: *the great apes; Numa the lion; La, Queen of Opar, the
Lost City.*

They had listened to his Frank David stories the same way:
the game warden rising from the black water beside a tree on a
moonless night, a tracker so keen he could see in the dark, could
follow a man through the deepest swamp by smelling the fear in
his sweat: a bent-over shadow stealing between the beaver lodges,
the cypress trees, the tangle of limb and vine, parting the long
wet bangs of Spanish moss with his rifle barrel, creeping toward
the glowing windows of the poacher's cabin, the deer hides nailed
to the wall, the gator pelts, the fish with their grim smiles hooked
to a clothesline, turtle shells like army helmets drying on the
windowsills. Any pit bull meant to guard the place lying behind
him with its throat slit, Frank David slips out of the fog with fog
still clinging to the brim of his hat. He circles the cabin, peers in

each window, mounts the porch. Puts his shoulder through the front door. Stands with wood splinters landing on the floor at his feet. A man of average height, clean-shaven: no threat until the big hands come up, curl into fists, the knuckles scarred, blue, sharp.

Kirxy finished his drink and poured another. It burned pleasantly in his belly. He looked at Neil and Dan, occupied by their bags of corn curls. A Merle Haggard song ended on the radio and Kirxy clicked it off, sparing the boys the evening news.

In the quiet, Kirxy heard Goodloe's truck. He glanced at Kent, who'd probably been hearing it for a while. Outside, Goodloe slammed his door. He hurried up the steps and tapped on the window. Kirxy exaggerated his limp and took his time letting him in.

"Good evening," Goodloe said, shaking the water from his hands. He took off his hat and hung it on the nail by the door, then hung up his yellow slicker.

"Evening, Sugarbaby," Kirxy said.

"If I can volunteer a little understatement here," Goodloe said, "it's a tad wet tonight."

"Yep." Kirxy went behind the counter and refilled his glass. "You just caught the tail end of happy hour. That is, if you're off the wagon again. Can I sell you a tonic? Warm you up?"

"You know we're a dry county, Kirxy."

"Would that be a no?"

"It's a watch your ass." Goodloe looked at the brothers. "Just wanted to ask these boys some questions."

"Have at it, Sugarbaby."

Goodloe walked to the Lance rack and detached a package of Nip-Chee crackers. He opened it, offered the pack to each of the boys. Only Dan took one. Smiling, Goodloe bit a cracker in half

146

and turned a chair around and sat with his elbows across its back. He looked over toward Kent, half-hidden by shadow. He chewed slowly. "Come on out here so I can see you, boy. I ain't gonna bite nothing but these stale-ass cheese crackers."

Kent moved a step closer, his eyes down, focused on Goodloe's boots.

Goodloe took out a notepad. "Where was y'all between the hours of four and eight A.M. two days ago?"

Kent looked at Neil. "Asleep."

"Asleep," Neil said.

Goodloe snorted. "Now come on, boys. The whole dern county knows y'all ain't slept a night in your life. Y'all was out on the river, weren't you? Making a few telephone calls?"

"You saying he's a liar?" Kirxy asked.

"I'm posing the questions here." Goodloe chewed another cracker. "Hell, everybody knows them other game wardens has been letting y'all get away with all kinds of shit. I reckon this dead fellow had something to prove. Being new and all."

"Sounds like he oughta used a life jacket," Kirxy said, wiping the counter.

"It appears"—Goodloe studied Kent—"that he might've been strangled. You got a alibi, boy?"

Kent lowered his eyes. Took his hands out of his pockets, balled them into fists.

Goodloe sighed. "I mean—Christ—is there anybody can back up what you're saying?"

The windows flickered.

"Yeah," Kirxy said. "I can."

Goodloe turned and faced the storekeeper. "You."

"That's right. They were here with me. Here in the store."

Goodloe looked amused. "They was, was they? Okay, Mr.

Kirxy. How come you didn't mention that to me this morning? Saved us all a little time?"

Kirxy sought Kent's eyes but saw nothing there, no under-standing, no appreciation. No fear. He went back to wiping the counter. "Well, I guess because they was passed out drunk, and I didn't want to say anything, being as I was, you know, giving alcohol to young'uns."

"But now that it's come down to murder, you figured you'd better just own up."

"Something like that."

Goodloe stared at Kirxy for a long time; neither would look away. Then the sheriff turned to the boys. "Y'all ever heard of Frank David?"

Dan nodded.

"Well," Goodloe said. "Looks like he's aiming to be this dis-trict's game warden. I figure he pulled some strings, what he did."

Kirxy came from behind the counter. "That all your questions? It's past closing and these young'uns need to go home and get some sleep." He went to the door and opened it, stood waiting.

"All righty then," the sheriff said, standing. "I expect I oughta be getting back to the office anyhow." He winked at Kirxy. "See you or these boys don't leave the county for a few days. This ain't over yet." He put the crackers in his coat. "I expect y'all might be hearing from Frank David, too," he said, watching the boys' faces. But there was nothing to see.

Alone later, Kirxy put out the light and bolted the door. He went to adjust the stove and found himself staring out the win-dow, looking into the dark where he knew the river was rising and swirling, tires and plastic garbage can lids and deadwood from upriver floating past. He struck a match and lit a cigarette, the glow of his ash reflected in the window, and he saw himself years ago, telling the boys those stories.

How Frank David would sit so still in the woods waiting for poachers that dragonflies would perch on his nose, gnats would walk over his eyeballs. Nobody knew where he came from, but Kirxy had heard he'd been orphaned as a baby in a fire and found half-starved in the swamp by a Cajun woman. She'd raised him on the slick red clay banks of the Tombigbee River, among lean black poachers and moonshiners. He didn't even know how old he was, people said. And they said he was the best poacher ever, the craftiest, the meanest. That he cut a drunk logger's throat in a juke joint knife fight one night. That he fled south and, underage, joined the marines in Mobile and wound up in Korea, the infantry, where because of his shooting ability and his stealth they made him a sniper. Before he left that country, he'd registered over a hundred kills, communists half a world away who never saw him coming.

Back home in Alabama, he disappeared for a few years, then showed up at the state game warden's office, demanding a job. Some people had heard that in the intervening time he'd gotten religion.

"What makes you think I ought to hire you?" the head warden asked him.

"Because I spent ten years of my life poaching right under your damn nose," Frank David said.

The Gates boys' pickup was the same old Ford their father had shot himself in several years before, heartbroken over their mother's death. The bullet hole in the roof had rusted out but was now covered with a strip of duct tape from Kirxy's store. Spots of the truck's floor were rusted away, too, so things in the road often flew up into their laps: rocks, Budweiser cans, a king snake they were trying to run over. The truck was older than any of them, only one thin prong left of the steering wheel and the holes of missing knobs in the dash. It was a three-speed, a column shifter, the gear stick covered with a buck's dried ball sack. The windows and windshield, busted or shot out years before, hadn't been replaced because most of their driving took them along back roads after dark or in fields, and the things they came upon were easier shots without glass.

Though he'd never had a license, Kent drove, had since he was eight. Neil rode shotgun. Tonight both were drinking, and in the back Dan stood holding his rifle and trying to keep his balance. Below the soles of his boots the floor was soft, a tarry black from the blood of all the animals they'd killed. You could see spike antlers, forelegs and hooves of deer. Teeth, feathers and fur. The brittle beaks and beards of turkeys and the delicate, hinged leg bone of something molded in the sludge like a fossil.

Just beyond a no-trespassing sign already gnawed up by bullets, Kent swerved off the road and they bounced and slid through a field in the rain, shooting at rabbits. Then they split up, the younger boys checking traps, one on each side of the river, and Kent in the boat rebaiting their trotlines the way his father had shown him.

They met at the truck just before midnight, untied the dogs and tromped over a steep logging path, Dan on one end of four leashes and the lunging hounds on the other. When they got to the bottomland, he unclipped the leashes and loosed the dogs and the brothers followed the baying ahead in the dark, aiming their flashlights into the black mesh of trees where the eyes of coons and possums gleamed like rubies. The hounds bayed and frothed, clawed the trunks of trees and leaped into the air and landed and leaped again, their sides pumping, ribs showing.

When the Gateses came to the river two hours later, the dogs were lapping water and panting. Dan bent and rubbed their ears and let them lick his cheeks. His brothers rested and drank, belching at the sky. After a time, they leashed the hounds and staggered downstream to the live oak where their boat was tied. They loaded the dogs in and shoved off into the fog and trolled over the still water.

In the middle, Neil lowered the wire and the chain—stolen from a child's swing set—behind the boat and began cranking the old telephone, which he held between his legs. Dan netted the stunned catfish (you couldn't touch them with your hand or they'd come to) and threw them into the cooler, where in a few seconds the waking fish would begin to thrash. In the rear, Kent propped his rifle on his knees and watched the bank in case a coyote wandered down hunting bullfrogs.

They climbed out of the woods into a dirt road in the misty dawn, plying through the muddy yards and pissing by someone's front porch in plain sight of the face inside. A few houses down, Morrisette didn't come to his door, and when Kent tried the handle it was locked. He looked at Neil, then put his elbow through the glass and reached in and unlocked it.

While his brothers searched for the liquor, Dan ate the biscuits he found wrapped in tinfoil on the stove. He found a box of cornflakes in a cabinet and ate most of them, too. He ate a plate of cold fried liver. Neil was in a bedroom looking under the bed. In the closet. He was going through drawers, his dirty fingers smudging the white shirts. In the back of the house Kent found the bathroom door, locked from the inside. He jimmied it open with his knife, and when he came into the kitchen, he had a gallon jar of whisky under his arm and Euphrates's stepdaughter by the wrist.

Dan stopped chewing, crumbs falling from his mouth. He approached the girl and put his hand out to touch her, but Kent pushed him hard, into the wall. Dan stayed there, a clock ticking beside his head, a string of spit linking his opened lips, watching as his brother ran his rough hands up and down the girl's shivering body, thumbing the nipples that showed through her shirt. Her eyes were closed, lips trembling in prayer. Looking down, Kent saw the puddle spreading around her bare feet. Dan giggled, then put his hand over his mouth.

"Shit," Kent said, letting her go. "Pissed herself."

She shrank back against the wall, behind the door.

And was still there, along with a bag of catfish on the table, when her stepfather came back half an hour later, ten gallons of whisky under the tarp in his truck.

On that same Saturday Kirxy drove to the chicken fights, held in Heflin Bradford's bulging barn, deep in woods cloudy with mosquitoes. He passed the hand-painted sign that'd been there forever, as long as he could remember, nailed to a tree. It said JESUS IS NOT COMING.

Kirxy climbed out of his truck and buttoned his collar, his ears full of cotton. Heflin's wife worked beneath a rented awning, grilling chicken and sausages, selling Cokes and beer. Gospel music played from a portable radio by her head. Heflin's grandson Nolan took the price of admission at the barn door and stamped the backs of white hands and the cracked pink palms of black ones. Men in overalls and baseball caps that said CAT DIESEL

POWER or STP stood at the tailgates of their pickups, smoking cigarettes, stooping to peer into the cages where roosters paced. The air was filled with windy rain spits and the crowing of roosters, the ground littered with limp dead birds.

A group of loggers was discussing Frank David, and Kirxy paused to listen.

"He's the one caught that bunch over in Warshington County," one man said. "Them alligator poachers."

"Sugarbaby said two of 'em wound up in the intensive care," another claimed. "Said they pulled a gun and old Frank David went crazy with a ax handle."

Kirxy moved on and paid the five-dollar admission. In the barn, there were bleachers along the walls and a big circular wooden fence in the center, a dome of chicken wire over the top. Kirxy found a seat at the bottom next to the back door, near a group of mean old farts he'd known for forty years. People around them called out bets and bets were accepted. Cans of beer lifted. Kirxy produced a thermos of coffee and a dented tin cup. He poured the coffee, then added whisky from a bottle that went back into his coat pocket. The tin cup warmed his fingers as he squinted through his bifocals to see which bird to bet on.

In separate corners of the barn, two bird handlers doused their roosters' heads and asses with rubbing alcohol to make them fight harder. They tightened the long steel curved spurs. When the referee in the center of the ring indicated it was time, the handlers entered the pen, each cradling his bird in his arms. They flashed the roosters at one another until their feathers had ruffled with blood lust and rage, the roosters pedaling the air, stretching their necks toward each other. The handlers kept them a breath apart for a second, then withdrew them to their corners, whispering in their ears. When the referee tapped the ground three times with his stick, the birds were unleashed. They charged and rose in the center of the ring, gouging with spur and beak, the handlers circling the fight like crabs, blood on their forearms and faces, ready to seize their roosters at the referee's cry of "Handle!"

A clan of Louisiana Cajuns watched. They'd emerged red-eyed from a van in a marijuana cloud: skinny, shirtless men with oily ponytails and goatees and tattoos of symbols of black magic. Under their arms, they carried thick white hooded roosters to pit against the reds and blacks of the locals. Their women had stumbled out of the van behind them, high yellow like gypsies, big-lipped, big-chested girls in halter tops tied at their bellies and miniskirts and moccasins.

In the ring the Cajuns kissed their birds on the beaks, and one tall, completely bald Cajun wearing gold earrings in both ears put his bird's whole head in his mouth. His girl, too, came barefoot into the ring, tattoo of a snake on her shoulder, and took the bird's head into her mouth.

"Bet on them white ones," a friend whispered to Kirxy. "These ones around here ain't ever seen a white rooster. They don't know what they're fighting."

That evening, bending to check a trap in the woods north of the river, Dan took hold of a sapling and yelped when a spray of water rained on him. He crouched, dripping, and waited while the drumming of his heart slowed. Forced himself to rise and move on so his brothers wouldn't laugh at him for being afraid.

Near dark, in a wooden trap next to an old fence row, he was surprised to find the tiny white fox they'd once seen cross the road in front of their truck. He squatted before the trap and poked a stick through the wire at the thin snout, his hand steady despite the way the fox snapped at the stick and bit off the end. Would the witch woman want this alive? At the thought of her, he looked around. It felt like she was watching him, as if she were hiding in a tree in the form of some animal, a possum or a swamp rat or a chicken snake. He stood and dragged the trap through the mud and over the land while in the trap the fox jumped in circles, growling.

A mile upstream, Neil had lost a boot to the mud and was hopping back one-footed to retrieve it. It stood buried to the ankle. He wrenched it free, then sat with his back against a sweet gum to scrape off the mud. He'd begun to lace the boot when he saw a hollow tree stump, something moving inside. With his rifle barrel he rolled the thing out—it was most of the body of a dead catfish, the movement from the maggots devouring it. When he kicked it, they spilled from the fish like rice pellets and lay throbbing in the mud.

Downstream, as night came and the rain fell harder, Kent trolled their boat across the river, flashlight in his mouth, using a stick to pull up a trotline length by length and removing the fish or turtles and rebaiting the hooks and dropping them back into the water. Near the bank, approaching the last hook, he heard something. He looked up with the flashlight in his teeth to see the thing untwirling in the air. It wrapped around his neck like a rope, and for an instant he thought he was being hanged. He grabbed the thing. It flexed and tightened, then his neck burned and went numb and he felt dizzy, his fingertips buzzing, legs weak, a tree on the bank distorting, doubling, tripling into a whole line of fuzzy shapes, turning sideways, floating.

Kent blinked. Felt his eyes bulging, his tongue swelling. His head about to explode. Then a bright light.

*   *   *

His brothers found the boat at dawn, four miles downstream, lodged on the far side in a fallen tree. They exchanged a glance, then looked back across the river. A heavy gray fog hooded the water and the boat appeared and dissolved in the ghostly limbs around it. Neil sat on a log and took off his boots and left them standing by the log. He removed his coat and laid it over the boots. He handed his brother his rifle without looking at him, left him watching as he climbed down the bank and, hands and elbows in the air like a believer, waded into the water.

Dan propped the second rifle against a tree and stood on the bank holding his own gun, casting his frightened eyes up and down the river. From far away a woodpecker drummed. Crows began to collect in a pine tree downstream. After a while Dan squatted, thinking of their dogs, tied to the bumper of their truck. They'd be under the tailgate, probably, trying to keep dry.

Soon Neil had trolled the boat back across. Together they pulled it out of the water and stood looking at their brother, who lay across the floor among the fish and turtles he'd caught. One greenish terrapin, still alive, a hook in its lip, stared back. They both knew what they were supposed to think—the blood and the sets of twin fang marks, the black bruises and shriveled skin, the neck swollen like mumps, the purple bulb of tongue between his lips. They were supposed to think *cottonmouth*. Kent's hands were squeezed into fists and they'd hardened that way, the skin wrinkled, his eyes half open. His rifle lay unfired in the boat, and the telephone rig seemed untouched, as if indeed a snake had done this.

But it wasn't the tracks of a snake they found when they went to get the white fox. The fox was gone, the trap empty, its catch sprung. Neil knelt and ran his knuckles along the rim of a boot print in the mud—not a very wide track, not very far from the next one. He put his finger in the black water that'd already begun to fill the track: not too deep. He looked up at Dan. The print of an average-sized man. In no hurry. Neil rose and they began.

Above them, the sky cracked and flickered.

Silently, quickly—no time to get the dogs—they followed the trail back through the woods, losing it once, twice, backtracking, working against the rain that fell and fell harder, that puddled blackly and crept up their legs, until they stood in water to their ankles, rain beading on the brims of their caps. They gazed at the ground, the sky, at the rain streaming down each other's muddy faces.

At the truck, Dan jumped into the driver's seat and reached for the keys. Neil appeared in the window, shaking his head. When Dan didn't scoot over, the older boy hit him in the jaw through the window, then slung open the door and pulled Dan out, sent him rolling over the ground. Neil climbed in and had trouble getting the truck choked. By the time he had the hang of it, Dan had gotten into the back and sat among the wet dogs, staring at his dead brother's eyes.

At their cabin, they carried Kent into the woods. They laid him on the ground and began digging near where their sister, mother and father were buried in their unmarked graves. For three hours they worked, the dogs coming from under the porch and sniffing around Kent and whining and watching the digging, finally slinking off and crawling back under the porch. An hour later they came out again and stood in a group at the edge of the yard, baying. The boys paused but saw or heard nothing. When the dogs kept making noise, Neil got his rifle and fired into the woods several times. He nodded to his brother and they went back to digging.

By the time they'd finished, it was late afternoon and the hole was full of slimy water and they were black with mud. They each took off one of Kent's boots and Neil got the things from his pockets. They stripped off his shirt and pants and socks and lowered him naked into the hole. When he bobbed to the top of the water, they got stones and weighted him down. Then shoveled mud into the grave.

They showed up at Esther's, black as tar.

"Where's Kent?" she asked, holding her robe closed at her throat.

"We buried him," Neil said, moving past her into the kitchen. She put a hand over her mouth, and as Neil told her what they'd found she slumped against the door, looking outside. An owl flew past in the floodlights. She thought of calling Kirxy but decided to wait until morning—the old bastard thought she was a slut and a corruption. For tonight she'd just keep them safe in her house.

Neil went to the den. He turned on the TV, the reception bad because of the weather. Dan, a bruise on his left cheek, climbed the stairs. He went into one of the bedrooms and closed the door behind him. It was chilly in the room and he noticed pictures of people on the wall, children and a tall man and a younger woman he took to be Esther. She'd been pretty then. He stood dripping on the floor, looking into her black-and-white face, searching for signs of the woman he knew now. Soon the door opened behind him and she came in. And though he still wore his filthy wet clothes, she steered him to the bed and guided him down onto the edge of it. She unbuckled his belt, removed his hunting knife, and stripped the belt off. She unbuttoned his shirt and rubbed her fingers across his chest, the hair just beginning to thicken there. She undid his pants and ran the zipper down its track. She worked them over his thighs, knees and ankles and draped them across the back of a chair. She pulled off his boots and socks. Pushed him back onto the bed. Pried a finger beneath the elastic of his underwear, felt what had already happened.

He looked at her face. His mouth opened. Esther touched his chin, the scratch of whiskers, his breath on her hand.

"Hush now," she said, and watched him fall asleep.

Downstairs, the TV went off.

When Goodloe knocked, Esther answered, a cold sliver of her face in the cracked door. "The hell you want?"

"Good evening to you, too. The Gateses here?"

"No."

Goodloe glanced behind him. "I believe that's their truck. It's kinda hard to mistake, especially for us trained lawmen. We was just cruising by and seen it."

She tried to close the door but Goodloe had his foot in it. He glanced at the three deputies who stood importantly by the Blazer. They dropped their cigarettes and crushed them out. They unsnapped their holsters and strode across the yard, standing behind Goodloe with their hands on their revolvers and their legs apart like TV deputies.

"Why don't y'all just let 'em alone?" Esther said. "Ain't they been through enough?"

"Tell 'em I'd like to see 'em," Goodloe said. "Tell 'em get their boots."

"You just walk straight to hell, mister."

Dan appeared behind her, lines from the bed linen on his face.

"Whoa, Nellie," Goodloe said. "Boy, you look plumb terrible. Why don't you let us carry you on down to the office for a little coffee. Little cake." He glanced back at one of the deputies. "We got any of that cinnamon roll left, Dave?"

"You got a warrant for their arrest?" Esther asked.

"No, I ain't got a warrant for their arrest. They ain't under arrest. They fixing to get questioned, is all. Strictly informal." Goodloe winked. "You reckon you could do without 'em for a couple of hours?"

"Fuck you, Sugarbaby."

The door slammed. Goodloe nodded down the side of the house and two deputies went to make sure nobody escaped from the back. But in a minute Dan came out dressed, his hands in his pockets, and followed Goodloe down the stairs, the deputies watching him closely, and watching the house.

"Where's your brothers?" Goodloe asked.

He looked down.

Goodloe nodded to the house and two deputies went in, guns drawn. They came out a few minutes later, frowning.

"Must've heard us coming," Goodloe said. "Well, we got this one. We'll find them other two tomorrow." They got into the Blazer and Goodloe looked at Dan, sitting in the back.

"Put them cuffs on him," Goodloe said.

Holding his rifle, Neil came out of the woods when the Blazer was gone. He returned to the house.

"They got Dan," Esther said. "Why didn't you come tell him they was out there?"

"Boy got to learn," Neil said. He went to the cabinet where she kept the whisky and took the bottle. She watched him go to the sofa and sit down in front of the blank TV. Soon she joined him, bringing glasses. He filled both, and when they emptied them he filled them again.

They spent the night like that, and at dawn they were drunk. Wearing her robe, Esther began clipping her fingernails, a cigarette smoking in the ashtray beside her. She'd forgotten about calling Kirxy.

Neil was telling her about the biggest catfish they'd ever called up: a hundred pounds, he swore, a hundred fifty. "You could of put your whole head in that old cat's mouth," he said, sipping his whisky. "Back fin long as your damn arm."

He stood. Walked to the front window. There were toads in the yard—with the river swelling they were everywhere. In the evenings there were rainfrogs. The yard had turned into a pond and each night the rainfrogs sang. It was like no other sound. Esther said it kept her up at night.

"That, and some other things," she said.

Neil heard a fingernail land in the ashtray. He rubbed his hand across his chin, felt the whiskers there. He watched the toads as they huddled in the yard, still as rocks, bloated and miserable-looking.

"That catfish was green," he said, sipping. "I swear before God. Green as grass."

"Them goddamn rainfrogs," she said. "I just lay there at night with my hands over my ears."

A clipping rang the ashtray.

He turned and went to her on the sofa. "They was moss growing on his nose," he said, putting his hand inside her robe, on her knee.

"Go find your brother," she said. She got up and walked unsteadily across the floor and went into the bathroom, closed the door. When she came out, he and the bottle were gone.

Without Kent, Neil felt free to do what he wanted, which was to drive very fast. He got the truck started and spun off, aiming for every mud hole he could. He shot past a house with a washing machine on the front porch, two thin black men butchering a hog hanging from a tree. One of the men waved with a knife. Drinking, Neil drove through the mountains of trash at the dump and turned the truck in circles, kicking up muddy rooster tails. He swerved past the Negro church and the graveyard where a group of blacks huddled, four wobbling poles over an open grave, the wind tearing the preacher's hat out of his hands and a woman's umbrella reversing.

When he tired of driving, he left the truck in their hiding place, and using trees for balance, stumbled down the hill to their boat. He carried Kent's rifle, which he'd always admired, and he wore Kent's jacket. On the river, he fired up the outboard and accelerated, the boat prow lifting and leveling out, the buzz of the motor rising in the trees. The water was nearly orange from mud, the cypress knees nothing but knobs and tips because of the floods, a cottonmouth wound around most every one. Nearing the old train trestle, he cut the motor and coasted to a stop. He sat listening to the rain, to the distant barking of a dog, half a mile away. Chasing something, maybe a deer. As the dog charged through the woods, Neil closed his eyes and imagined the terrain, marking where he thought the dog was now and where he thought it was now. Then the barking stopped, suddenly, as if the dog had run smack into a tree.

Neil clicked on the trolling motor and moved the boat close to the edge of the river, the rifle across his knees. He scanned the banks, and when the rain started to fall harder he accelerated toward the trestle. From beneath the cross ties, he smelled creosote and watched the rain as it stirred the river. He looked into the gray trees and thought he would drive into town later, see about getting Dan. Kent had never wanted to go to Grove Hill— their father had warned them of the police, of jail. In town your truck needed to have a tag and taillights that worked.

Neil picked up one of the catfish from the night before. It was cold and stiff, as if carved out of wood. He stared at it, watching the green blowflies hover above his fist, then threw it over into the weeds along the bank.

The telephone rig was under the seat. He lifted the chain quietly, considering what giant catfish might be passing beneath the boat this very second, a thing as large as a man's thigh with eyes the size of ripe plums and skin the color of mud. Catfish, their father had taught them, have long whiskers that make them the only fish you can "call." Kirxy had told Neil and his brothers that if a game warden caught you telephoning, all you needed to do was dump your box overboard. But, Kirxy warned, Frank David would handcuff you and jump overboard and swim around the bottom of the river until he found your rig.

Neil spat a stream of tobacco juice into the water. Minnows appeared and began to investigate, nibbling at the dark yolk of spit as it elongated and dissolved. With the rifle's safety off, he lowered the chain into the water, then the wire, a good distance apart. He checked the connections, then lifted the phone and began to crank. "Hello?" he whispered, the thing his father had always said, grinning in the dark. The wind picked up a bit, he heard it rattling in the trees, and he dialed faster, had just seen the first silver body appear behind him when something landed with a clatter in the boat. He glanced over.

A bundle of dynamite, sparks hissing off the end, fuse already gone. He looked above him, the trestle, but nobody was there. He moved to grab the dynamite, but his cheeks ballooned with hot red wind and his hands caught fire.

When the smoke cleared and the water stopped boiling, silver bodies began to bob to the surface—largemouth bass, bream, gar, suckers, white perch, pollywogs, catfish—some only stunned but others dead, in pieces, pink fruitlike things, the water blooming darkly with mud.

Kirxy's telephone rang for the second time in one day, a rarity that proved what his wife had always said: bad news comes over the phone. The first call had been Esther, telling him of Kent's death, Dan's arrest, Neil's disappearance. This time Kirxy heard Goodloe's voice tell him that somebody—or maybe a couple of somebodies—had been blown up out on the trestle.

"Neil," Kirxy said, sitting.

He arrived at the trestle, and with his cane hobbled over the uneven tracks. Goodloe's deputies and three ambulance drivers in rubber gloves and waders were scraping pieces off the cross ties with spoons, dropping the parts in Ziploc bags. The boat, two flattened shreds of aluminum, lay on the bank. In the water, minnows darted about, nibbling.

"Christ," Kirxy said. He brought a handkerchief to his lips. Then he went to where Goodloe stood on the bank, writing in his notebook.

"What do you aim to do about this?" Kirxy demanded.

"Try to figure out who it was, first."

"You know goddamn well who it was."

"I expect, judging from that boat over yonder, it's either Kent or Neil Gates."

"It's Neil," Kirxy said.

"How you know that?"

Kirxy told him that Kent was dead.

Goodloe studied the storekeeper. "I ain't seen the body. Have you?"

Kirxy's blood pressure was going up. "Fuck, Sugarbaby. Are you one bit aware what's going on here?"

"Fishing accident," Goodloe said. "His bait exploded."

From the bank, a deputy called that he'd found most of a boot. "Foot's still in it," he said, holding it up by the lace. The deputy behind him gagged and turned away.

"Tag it," Goodloe said, writing something down. "And keep looking. Puke on your own time."

Kirxy poked Goodloe in the shoulder with his cane. "You really think Neil'd blow himself up?"

Goodloe looked at his shoulder, the muddy cane print, then at the storekeeper. "Not on purpose, I don't." He paused. "Course, suicide does run in their family."

"You half-wit son of a bitch. What about Kent?"

"What about him?"

"Christ, Sugarbaby—"

Goodloe held up his hand. "Just show me, Kirxy."

They left the ambulance drivers and the deputies and walked the other way without talking. When they came to Goodloe's Blazer, they got in and drove without talking. Soon they stopped in front of the Gates cabin. Instantly hounds surrounded the

truck, barking viciously and jumping with muddy paws against
the glass. Goodloe blew the horn until the hounds slunk away,
heads low, fangs bared. The sheriff opened his window and fired
several times in the air, backing the dogs up.

Before he and Kirxy got out, Goodloe reloaded.

The hounds kept to the edge of the woods, watching, while
Kirxy led Goodloe behind the decrepit cabin. Rusty screens cov-
ered some windows, rags of drape others. Beneath the house, the
dogs paced them. "Back here," Kirxy said, heading into the trees.
Esther had said they'd buried Kent, and this was the logical place.
He went slowly, already out of breath, stopping to cough once.
Sure enough, there lay the grave. You could see where the dogs
had been scratching around it.

Goodloe went over and toed the dirt. "You know the cause of
death?"

"Yeah, dumb-ass, I know the cause of death. His name's Frank
fucking David."

"I meant how he was killed."

"The boys said snakebite. Three times in the neck. But I'd do
an autopsy."

"You would." Goodloe exhaled. "Okay. I'll send Roy and Av-
ery over here to dig his ass up. Maybe shoot these goddern dogs."

"I'll tell you what you better do first. You better keep Dan
locked up safe."

"I can't hold him much longer," Goodloe said. "Unless he
confesses."

Kirxy swung at him with his cane and nearly lost his balance.
At the edge of the woods the dogs tensed. Goodloe backed away,
raising his pistol, the grave between them.

"You crazy, Kirxy? You been locked in that store too long?"

"Goodloe," Kirxy gasped. The cotton in his left ear had come out and air was roaring through his head. "Even you can't be this stupid. You let that boy out and he's that cold-blooded fucker's next target—"

"*Target*, Kirxy? Shit. Ain't nothing to prove anybody killed them damn boys. This one snakebit, you said so yourself. That other one blowing his own self up. Them dern Gateses has fished with dynamite their whole life. You oughta know that—you the one gets it for 'em." He narrowed his eyes. "You're about neck deep in this damn thing, you know. And I don't mean just lying to protect them boys, neither. I mean selling explosives illegally, to minors, Kirxy."

"I don't give a shit if I am!" Kirxy yelled. "Two dead boys in two days and you're worried about dynamite? You oughta be out there looking for Frank David."

"He ain't supposed to be here for another week or two," Goodloe said. "Paperwork—"

He fired his pistol.

Kirxy jumped, looked down at his chest to see the blood, but the sheriff was aiming past him, and when Kirxy followed his eyes he saw the three-legged dog that had been creeping in. It lay slumped in the mud, a hind leg kicking, blood coloring the water around it.

Goodloe backed a step away, smoke curling from the barrel of his pistol.

Around them the other dogs circled, heads low, moving sideways, the hair on their spines sticking up.

"Let's argue about this in the truck," Goodloe said.

At the store Kirxy put out the OPEN sign. He sat in his chair with his coffee and a novel. He'd read the same page three times when it occurred to him to phone Montgomery and get Frank David's office on the line. It took a few calls, but he soon got the number and dialed. The snippy young woman who answered told Kirxy that yes, Mr. David *was* supposed to take over the Lower Peach Tree district, but that he wasn't starting until next week, she thought.

Where was he now? Kirxy wanted to know.

"Florida?" she said. "No, Louisiana. Fishing." No, sir, he couldn't be reached. He preferred his vacations private.

Kirxy slammed down the phone. He lit a cigarette and tried to think.

It was just a matter, he decided, of keeping Dan alive until Frank David officially took over the district. There were probably other game wardens who'd testify that Frank David was indeed over in Louisiana fishing right now. But once the son of a bitch *officially* moved here, he'd have a motive because he'd known the dead game warden, and his alibi wouldn't be as strong. If Dan turned up dead, Frank David would be the chief suspect. Even Goodloe'd be able to see that.

Kirxy inhaled smoke deeply and tried to imagine how Frank David would think. How he would act. The noise he would make or not make as he went through the woods. What he would say if you happened upon him. Or he upon you. What he would do if he came into the store. Certainly he wasn't the creature Kirxy had created to scare the boys, not some wild ghostly thing. He was just a man who'd had a hard life and who'd grown bitter and angry. A man who chose to uphold the law because breaking it was no challenge. A man with no obligation to any other men or a family. Just to himself and his job. To some goddamned un-written game warden code. His job was to protect the wild things the law had deemed worthy. Deer and turkeys. Alligators. But how did the Gates boys fall into the category of trash animal—wildcats or possums or armadillos, snapping turtles, snakes? Things you could kill any time, run over in your truck and not even look at in your mirror to see dying behind you? Christ. Why couldn't Frank David see that he, more than a match for the boys, was exactly the same as them?

Kirxy drove to the highway. The big thirty-aught-six he hadn't touched in years was on the seat next to him, and as he steered he pushed cartridges into the clip, then shoved the clip into the gun's underbelly. He pulled the lever that injected a cartridge into the chamber and took a long drink of whisky to wash down three of the pills that helped dull the ache in his knees, and the one in his gut.

It was almost dark when he arrived at the edge of a large field. He parked facing the grass. This was a place a few hundred yards from a fairly well-traveled blacktop, a spot no sane poacher would dare use. There were already two or three deer creeping into the open from the woods across the field. They came to eat the tall grass, looking up only when a car passed, their ears swiveling, jaws frozen, sprigs of grass twitching in their lips like the legs of insects.

Kirxy sat watching. He sipped his whisky and lit a cigarette with a trembling hand. Both truck doors were locked and he knew this was a very stupid thing he was doing. Several times he told himself to go home, let things unfold as they would. Then he saw the faces of the two dead boys. And the face of the live one.

When Boo had killed himself, the oldest two had barely been teenagers, but it was twelve-year-old Dan who'd found him. That truck still had window glass then, and half the back windshield had been sprayed red with blood. Flies had gathered at the top of the truck around what Dan discovered to be a bullet hole, the pistol still clenched in his father's hand. The rim of Boo's hat still on his head, the top blown out. Kirxy frowned, thinking of it. The back of the truck was full of wood Boo'd been cutting, and the three boys had unloaded the wood and stacked it neatly beside the road. Kirxy shifted in his seat, imagining the boys pushing that truck for two miles over dirt roads, somehow finding the leverage or whatever, the goddamn strength, to get it home. To pull their father from inside and bury him. To clean out the truck.

Kirxy shuddered and thought of Frank David, then made himself think of his wife instead. He rubbed his biceps and watched the shadows creep across the field, the tree line dimming, beginning to disappear.

Soon it was full dark. He unscrewed the interior lightbulb from the ceiling, rolled down the window, pulled the door lock up quietly. Holding his breath, he opened the door. Outside, he propped the rifle on the side mirror, flicked the safety off. He reached through the window, felt along the dash for the headlight switch, pulled it.

The field blazed with the eyes of deer—red hovering dots staring back at him. Kirxy aimed and squeezed the trigger at the first pair of eyes. Not waiting to see if he'd hit the deer, he moved the gun to another pair. He'd gotten off seven shots before the eyes began to vanish. When the last echo from the gun faded, at least three deer lay dead or wounded in the glow of headlights. One doe bleated weakly and bleated again. Kirxy coughed and took the gun back into the truck, closed the door and reloaded in the dark. Then he waited.

The doe kept bleating and things in the woods took shape, detached and whisked toward Kirxy over the grass like spooks.

And the little noises. Things like footsteps. And the stories. Frank David appearing in the bed of somebody's *moving* truck and punching through the back glass, grabbing and breaking the driver's arm. Leaping from the truck and watching while it wrecked.

"Quit it," Kirxy croaked. "You damn schoolgirl."

Several more times that night he summoned his nerve and flicked on the headlights, firing at any eyes he saw or thought he saw or firing at nothing. When he finally fell asleep at two A.M., his body numb with painkillers and whisky, he dreamed of his wife on the day of her first miscarriage. The way the nurses couldn't find the vein in her arm, how they'd kept trying with the needle, the way she'd cried and held his fingers tightly, like a woman giving birth.

He started awake, terrified, as if he'd fallen asleep driving.

Caring less for silence, he stumbled from the truck and flicked on the lights and fired, though now there were no eyes. He lowered the gun and for no good reason found himself thinking of a time when he'd tried fly fishing, standing in his yard with his wife watching from the porch, *Tarzan of the Apes* in her lap, him whipping the line in the air, showing off, and then the strange pulling you get when you catch a fish, and Betty jumping to her feet, the book falling, and her yelling that he'd caught a bat, for heaven's sake, a *bat!*

He climbed back into the truck. His hands shook so hard he had trouble getting the door locked. He bowed his head, missing her so much that he cried, softly, for a long time.

Dawn found him staring at a field littered with dead does, yearlings and fawns. One of the deer, only wounded, was trying to crawl toward the safety of the trees. Kirxy got out of the truck and vomited colorless water, then stood looking around at the foggy morning. He lifted his rifle and limped into the grass in the drizzle and, a quick hip shot, put the live deer out of its misery.

He was sitting on the open tailgate trying to light a cigarette when Goodloe and a deputy passed in their Blazer and stopped.

The sheriff stepped out, signaling for the deputy to stay put. He sat beside Kirxy on the tailgate, the truck dipping with his weight. His stomach was growling.

"You old fool," Goodloe said, staring at Kirxy and then behind them at the field. "You figured to make Frank David show himself?" He shook his head. "Good lord almighty, Kirxy. What'll it take to prove to you there ain't no dern vigilante game warden out there?"

Kirxy didn't answer. Goodloe went to the Blazer and told the deputy to pick him up at the old man's store. "Get Dave over here to load up them deer, quick," he said. "Tell him to gut 'em and drop 'em off at my place, in the barn."

The deputy put the Blazer into gear. "Can I have some tenderloins, boss?"

Goodloe slammed the door. At Kirxy's truck, he helped the old man into the passenger seat and went around and got in the driver's side. He took the rifle and unloaded it, put its clip in his pocket.

"We'll talk about them deer later," he said. "Now I better get you back."

They'd gone a silent mile when Kirxy said, "Would you mind running me by Esther's?"

Goodloe shrugged and turned that way. His stomach made a strangling noise and he patted it absently. The rain and wind were picking up, rocking the truck. The sheriff took a bottle of bourbon from his pocket. "Medicinal," he said, handing it to Kirxy.

"It's just been two freak accidents, is all, Kirxy. I seen some strange shit in my life, a lot stranger than this. Seen a nigger had rabies one time? All foaming at the mouth? Bit his dern wife on her titty fore she shot him. Hell of a thing, buddy boy." He took the bottle back. "Them Gateses is just a unlucky bunch. Period. I ain't one to go believing in curses, Kirxy, but I swear to God if they ain't just downright snakebit."

Soon Goodloe parked in front of Esther's and they sat waiting for the rain to slack. Kirxy rubbed his knees and looked out the windows where the bottoms of trees were submerged in the rising floodwaters.

"They say old Esther has her a root cellar," Goodloe said, taking a sip. "Shit. I expect it's full of water this time of year, ain't it? She's probably got cottonmouths wrapped around her plumbing." He shuddered and offered the bottle. Kirxy took it and sipped. He gave it back and Goodloe drank, then drank again. "Lord, if that don't hit the spot.

"When I was in the service," Goodloe went on, "over in Thailand? They had them little bitty snakes, them banded kraits, they called 'em. Poison as cobras, what they told us. Used to hide up under the commode lid. Every time you took you a shit, you had to lift up the lid, see was one there." He drank. "Yep. It was many a time I kicked one off in the water, flushed it down."

"Wait here," Kirxy said. He opened the door, his pants leg darkening as rain poured in, cold as needles. He set his knee out deliberately, planted his cane in the mud and pulled himself up, stood in water to his ankles. He limped across the yard with his hand before his face, blocking the rain. There were two chickens on the front porch, their feathers fluffed out so that they looked strange, menacing. Kirxy climbed the porch steps with the pain so strong in his knees that stars were popping near his face by the time he reached the top. He leaned against the house, breathing hard. Touched himself at the throat where a tie might've gone. Then he rapped gently with the hook of his cane. The door opened immediately. Dark inside. She stood there, looking at him.

"How come you don't ever stop by the store anymore?" he asked.

She folded her arms.

"Neil's dead," he said.

"I heard," Esther said. "And I'm leaving. Fuck this place and every one of you."

She closed the door and Kirxy would never see her again.

At the store, Goodloe nodded for the deputy to stay in the Blazer, then he took Kirxy by the elbow and helped him up the steps. He unlocked the door for the old man and held his icy hand as he sank in his chair.

"Want these boots off?" Goodloe asked, spreading a blanket over Kirxy's lap.

He bent and unlaced the left, then the right.

"Pick up your foot. Now the other one."

He set the wet boots by the stove.

"It's a little damp in here. I'll light this thing."

He found a box of kitchen matches on a shelf under the counter among the glass figurines Kirxy's wife had collected. The little deer. The figure skater. The unicorn. Goodloe got a fire going in the stove and stood warming the backs of his legs.

"I'll bring Dan by a little later," he said, but Kirxy didn't seem to hear.

Goodloe sat in his office with his feet on his desk, rolling a cartridge between his fingers. A plate of ribs sat untouched before him. Despite himself, he was beginning to wonder if Kirxy might be right. Maybe Frank David *was* out there on the prowl. Good lawman would at least consider the possibility. He stood, took off his pistol belt and walked to the back, pushed open the swinging door and had Roy buzz him through. So far he'd had zero luck getting anything out of Dan. The boy just sat in his cell wrapped in a blanket, his head shaved for lice, not talking to anybody, not eating. Goodloe had told him about his brother's death, and he'd seen no emotion cross the boy's face. Goodloe figured that it wasn't this youngest one who'd killed that game warden; it'd probably been the other two. He knew that this boy wasn't carrying a full cylinder, the way he never talked, but most likely he had been a witness. Goodloe had even considered calling a psychologist from the Searcy Mental Hospital to give the boy an evaluation.

"Come on," Goodloe said, stopping by Dan's cell and jingling his keys. "I'm fixing to put your talent to some good use."

He kept the boy cuffed as the deputy drove them toward the trestle.

"Turn your head, Dave," Goodloe said, handing Dan a pint of Old Crow. The boy took it in both hands and unscrewed the lid, began to drink too fast.

"Slow down there, partner," Goodloe said, taking back the bottle. "You need to be a little bit alert."

Soon they stood near the trestle, gazing at the flat shape of the boat on the bank. Dan knelt and examined the ground. The deputy came up and started to say something, but Goodloe motioned for quiet.

"Just like a goddern bloodhound," he whispered. "Maybe I ought give him your job."

"Reckon what he's after?" the deputy asked.

Dan scrabbled up the trestle, and the two men followed. The boy walked slowly over the rails, first staring into the trees, then examining the spaces between the cross ties. He stopped, bent down and peered at something. Picked it up.

"What you got there, boy?" Goodloe called, going and squatting beside him. He took a sip of Old Crow.

When Dan hit him, two-handed, the bottle flew one way and Goodloe the other. Both landed in the river, Goodloe with his hand clapped to his head to keep his hat on. He came up immediately, bobbing and sputtering. On the trestle, the deputy tackled Dan and they went down fighting on the cross ties. Below, Goodloe dredged himself out of the water. He came ashore dripping and tugged his pistol from its holster. He held it up so that a thin trickle of orange water fell. He took off his hat and looked up to see the deputy disappear belly-first into the face of the river.

Dan sprinted down the track, toward the swamp. The deputy came boiling ashore. He had his own pistol drawn and was looking around vengefully.

Goodloe climbed the trestle in time to see Dan disappear into the woods. The sheriff chased him for a while, ducking limbs and vines, but stopped, breathing hard, his hand on his side, his cheeks red.

. . .

Dan circled back through the woods and went quickly over the soft ground, scrambling up the sides of hills and sliding down the other sides. Two hollows over, he heard the deputy heading in the wrong direction. Dan slowed a little and trotted for a long time in the rain, the cuffs rubbing his wrists raw. He stopped and looked at what he'd been carrying in one hand: a match, limp and black now with water, nearly dissolved. He stood looking at the trees around him, the hanging Spanish moss and the cypress knees rising from the stagnant creek to his left.

The hair on the back of his neck rose. He knelt, tilting his head, closing his eyes, and listened. He heard the rain, heard it hit leaves and wood and heard the puddles lapping at their tiny banks, but beyond those sounds there were other sounds. A mockingbird mocking a blue jay. A squirrel barking and another answering. The deputy falling, a quarter mile away. Then another sound, this one close. A match striking.

Dan began to run before opening his eyes and crashed into a tree. He rolled to his feet and ran again, tearing through limbs and briars and spiderwebs. He leapt small creeks and slipped and got up and kept running. At every turn he expected Frank David, and he was near tears when he finally stumbled into his family graveyard.

The first thing he saw was that Kent had been dug up. Wooden stakes surrounded the hole and fenced it in with yellow tape that had words on it. Dan approached slowly, his fists under his chin. Something floated in the grave. With his heart pounding, he peered inside. It was the big three-legged hound.

Wary of the trees behind him, he crept toward their backyard, stopping at the edge. He crouched and blew into his hands to warm his cheeks. He gazed at the dark windows of their cabin, then circled the house, keeping to the woods. He saw the pine tree with the low limb they used for stringing up larger animals to clean, the rusty chain hanging and the iron pipe they stuck through the back legs of a deer or the rare wild pig. Kent and Neil had usually done the cleaning while Dan fed the guts to their dogs and tried to keep them from fighting.

And there, past the tree, scattered, lay the rest of the dogs. Shot dead. Partially eaten. Buzzards standing in the mud, staring boldly at him with their heads bloody and their beaks open.

It was dark when Kirxy woke in his chair, he'd heard the door creak. Someone stood there, and the storekeeper was afraid until he smelled the river.

"Hey, boy," he said.

Dan ate two cans of potted meat with his fingers and a candy bar and a box of saltines. Kirxy gave him a Coke from the red cooler and he drank it and took another one while Kirxy got a hacksaw from the rack of tools behind the counter. He slipped the cardboard wrapping off and nodded for Dan to sit. The storekeeper pulled up another chair and faced the boy and began sawing the handcuff chain. The match dropped out of Dan's hand but neither saw it. Dan sat with his head down and his palms up, his wrists on his knees, breathing heavily, while Kirxy worked and the silver shavings accumulated in a pile between their boots. The boy didn't lift his head the entire time, and he'd been asleep for quite a while when Kirxy finally sawed through. The old man rose, flexing his sore hands, and got a blanket from a shelf. He unfolded it, shook out the dust and spread it over Dan. He went to the door and turned the dead bolt.

The phone rang later. It was Goodloe, asking about the boy and telling what had happened.

Kirxy nearly smiled. "You been lost all this time, Sugarbaby?"

"Reckon I have," Goodloe admitted, "and we still ain't found Deputy Dave yet."

For a week they stayed in the store together. At times Kirxy could barely walk, and other times the pain in his side was worse than ever. He gave the boy a stocking cap to cover his skinned head and put him to work, sweeping, dusting and scrubbing the shelves. He had Dan pull a table next to his chair, and Kirxy did something he hadn't done in years: took inventory. With the boy's help, he counted and ledgered each item, marking it in his long green book. The back shelf contained canned soups, vegetables, sardines and tins of meat. Many of the cans were so old that the labels flaked off in Kirxy's hand, and so they were unmarked when Dan replaced them in the rings they'd made not only in the dust but on the wood itself. In the back of that last shelf, Dan discovered four tins of Underwood Deviled Ham, and as their labels fell away at Kirxy's touch, he remembered a time when he'd purposely unwrapped the paper from these cans because each label showed several red dancing devils, and some of his colored customers had refused to buy them.

Kirxy now understood that his store was dead, that it no longer provided a service. His colored customers had stopped coming years before. The same with Esther. For the past few years, except for an occasional hunter or logger, he'd been in business for the Gates boys alone. He looked across the room at Dan, spraying a window with Windex and wiping at it absently, gazing outside.

The boy wore the last of the new denim overalls Kirxy had in stock, and they were too short by an inch or two. Once, when the store had thrived, he'd had many sizes, but for the longest time now the only ones he'd stocked were the boys'.

That night, beneath his standing lamp, Kirxy began again to read his wife's copy of *Tarzan of the Apes* to Dan. He sipped his whisky and spoke clearly, to be heard over the rain. When he paused to turn a page, he saw that the boy lay asleep across the row of chairs they'd arranged in the shape of a bed. Looking down through his bifocals, Kirxy flipped to the front of the book and saw his wife's name written in her neat script. He moved his thumb over it and read it to himself. Then he turned to the back of the book to the list of other Tarzan novels—twenty-four in all—and he decided to order them through the mail so he and Dan would know the complete adventures of Tarzan of the Apes.

In the morning, Goodloe called and said that Frank David had officially arrived—the sheriff himself had witnessed the swearing-in—and he was now this district's game warden.

"Pretty nice old fellow," Goodloe said. "Kinda quiet. Polite. Asked me how the fishing was."

Then it's over, Kirxy thought.

A week later, Kirxy told Dan he had business in Grove Hill. He'd spent the night before trying to decide whether to take the boy with him but had decided not to, that he couldn't watch him forever. Besides, town wasn't the place for a Gates. Before he left he gave Dan his thirty-aught-six and told him to stay put, not to leave for anything. For himself, Kirxy took an old twenty-two bolt action and placed it in the back window rack of his truck. He waved to Dan and drove off.

He thought that if the boy wanted to run away, it was his own choice. Kirxy owed him the chance, at least.

At the doctor's office the tired-looking young surgeon frowned and removed his glasses when he told Kirxy that the cancer was advancing, that he'd need to check into the hospital in Mobile immediately. It was way past time. "Just look at your color," the surgeon said. Kirxy stood, thanked the man, put on his hat and limped outside. He went by the post office and placed his order for the Tarzan books. He shopped for supplies in the Dollar Store, using the buggy for support, and then the Piggly Wiggly, had the checkout boys put the boxes in the front seat beside him. Coming out of the drugstore, he remembered that it was Saturday, that there'd be chicken fights today. And possible news about Frank David.

At Heflin's, Kirxy paid his five-dollar admission and let Heflin help him to a seat in the bottom of the stands. He poured some whisky into his coffee and sat studying the crowd. Nobody had mentioned Frank David, but a few old-timers had offered their sympathies on the deaths of Kent and Neil.

Down in the pit the Cajuns were back, and during the eighth match—one of the Louisiana whites versus a local red, the tall bald Cajun stooping and circling the tangled birds and licking his lips as his rooster swarmed the other and hooked it, the barn smoky and dark, rain splattering the tin roof—the door swung open.

Instantly the crowd was hushed. Feathers settled to the ground. Even the Cajuns knew who he was. He stood at the door, unarmed, his hands on his hips. A wiry man. He lifted his chin and people tried to hide their drinks. His giant ears. That hooked nose. The eyes. Bird handlers reached over their shoulders, clawing at the numbered pieces of masking tape on their backs. The two handlers and the referee in the ring sidled out, leaving the roosters.

For a full minute Frank David stood staring. People stepped out the back door. Climbed out windows. Half-naked boys in the rafters were frozen like monkeys hypnotized by a snake.

Frank David's gaze didn't stop on Kirxy but settled instead on the roosters, the white one pecking at the red's eyes. Outside, trucks roared to life, backfiring like gunshots. Kirxy placed his hands on his knees. He rose, turned up his coat collar and flung his coffee out. Frank David still hadn't looked at him. Kirxy planted his cane and made his way painfully out the back door and through the mud.

Not a person in sight, just clattering tailgates vanishing into the woods.

From inside his truck, Kirxy watched Frank David walk away from the barn and head toward the trees. Watched him step around a mud puddle. Now he was just a blurry bowlegged man with white hair. Kirxy felt behind him for the twenty-two rifle with one hand while rolling down the window with the other. He had a little trouble aiming the gun with his shaky arms. He pulled back the bolt. He flicked the safety off. The sight of the rifle wavered between Frank David's shoulders as the game warden walked. As if an old storekeeper were nothing to fear.

Closing one eye, Kirxy pulled the trigger. He didn't hear the shot, though later he would notice his ears ringing.

Frank David's coat bloomed out to the side and he missed a step. He stopped and put his hand to his lower right side and looked over his shoulder at Kirxy, who was fumbling with the rifle's bolt action. Then Frank David was gone, just wasn't there, there were only the trees, bent in the rain, and shreds of fog in the air. For a moment Kirxy wondered if he'd seen a man at all, or if he'd shot at something out of his own imagination, if the cancer that had started in his pancreas had spread up along his spine into his brain and was deceiving him, forming men out of the air and walking them across fields, giving them hands and eyes and the power to disappear.

From inside the barn, a rooster crowed. Kirxy remembered Dan. He hung the rifle in its rack and started his truck, gunned the engine. He banged over the field, flattening saplings and a fence, and though he couldn't feel his feet, he drove very fast.

Not until two days later, in the VA hospital in Mobile, would Kirxy finally begin to piece it all together. Parts of that afternoon were patchy and hard to remember: shooting at Frank David, going to the store and finding it empty, no sign of a struggle, the thirty-aught-six gone, as if Dan had walked out on his own and taken the gun. Kirxy could remember getting back into his truck. He'd planned to drive to Grove Hill—the courthouse, the game warden's office—and find Frank David and finish the job, but somewhere along the way he blacked out behind the wheel and veered off the road into a ditch. He barely remembered the rescue workers and the lights and sirens. Goodloe himself pulling Kirxy out.

Later that night two coon hunters had stumbled across Dan, wandering along the riverbank, his face and shirt covered in blood, the thirty-aught-six nowhere to be found.

When Goodloe told the semiconscious Kirxy what happened, the storekeeper turned silently to the window, where he saw only the reflected face of an old, dying, failed man.

And later still, in the warm haze of morphine, Kirxy lowered his eyelids and let his imagination unravel and retwine the mystery of Frank David: it was as if Frank David himself appeared in the chair where Goodloe had sat, as if the game warden broke the seal on a bottle of Jim Beam and leaned forward on his elbows and touched the bottle to Kirxy's cracked lips and whispered to him a story about boots going over land and then a gunshot and rain washing the blood trail away even as the boots passed. About a tired old game warden taking his hand out of his coat and seeing the blood there, feeling it trickle along his side and down the back of his leg. About the boy in the game warden's truck, handcuffed, gagged, blindfolded. About driving carefully through deep ruts in the road. Stopping behind Esther's empty house and carrying the kicking wet boy inside on his shoulder.

When the blindfold is removed, Dan has trouble focusing but knows where he is because of her smell. Bacon and soap. Cigarettes, dust. Frank David holds what looks like a pillowcase. He comes across the room and puts the pillowcase down. He rubs his eyes and sits on the bed beside Dan. He puts on a pair of reading glasses and opens a book of matches and lights a cigarette. Holds the filtered end to Dan's lips, but the boy doesn't inhale. Frank David puts the cigarette in his own lips, the embers glow. Then he drops it on the floor, crushes it out with his boot. Picks up the butt and slips it into his shirt pocket. He puts his hand over the boy's watery eyes, the skin of his palm dry and hard. Cool. Faint smell of blood. He moves his fingers over Dan's nose, lips, chin. Stops at his throat and holds the boy tightly but not painfully. In a strange way Dan can't understand, he finds it reassuring. His thudding heart slows. Something is struggling beside his shoulder and Frank David takes the thing from the bag. Now the smell in the room changes. Dan begins to thrash and whip his head from side to side.

"Goddamn, son," Frank David whispers. "I hate to civilize you."

Goodloe began going to the veterans' hospital in Mobile once a week. He brought Kirxy cigarettes from his store. There weren't any private rooms available in the hospital, and the beds around the storekeeper were filled with dying ex-soldiers who never talked, but Kirxy was beside a window and Goodloe would raise the glass and prop it open with a novel. They smoked together and drank whisky from paper cups, listening for nurses.

It was the tall mean one.

"One more time, goddamn it," she said, coming out of nowhere and plucking the cigarettes from their lips so quickly they were still puckered.

Sometimes Goodloe would push Kirxy down the hall when they could get a wheelchair, the IV rack attached by a stainless steel contraption with a black handle the shape of a flower. They would go to the elevator and ride down three floors to a covered area where people smoked and talked about the weather. There were nurses and black cafeteria workers in white uniforms and hair nets and people visiting other people and a few patients. Occasionally in the halls they'd see some mean old fart Kirxy knew and they'd talk about hospital food or chicken fighting. Or the fact that Frank David had surprised everyone by deciding to retire after only a month of quiet duty, that the new game warden was from Texas. And a nigger to boot.

Then Goodloe would wheel Kirxy back along a long window, out of which they could see the tops of oak trees.

On one visit, Goodloe told Kirxy they'd taken Dan out of intensive care. Three weeks later he said the boy'd been discharged.

"I give him a ride to the store," Goodloe said. This was in late May and Kirxy was a yellow skeleton with hands that shook.

"I'll stop by and check on him every evening," Goodloe went on. "He'll be okay, the doctor says. Just needs to keep them bandages changed. I can do that, I reckon."

They were quiet then, for a time, just the coughs of the dying men and the soft swishing of nurses' thighs and the hum of IV machines.

"Goodloe," Kirxy whispered, "I'd like you to help me with something."

The sheriff leaned in to hear, an unlit cigarette behind his ear like a pencil.

Kirxy's tongue was white and cracked, his breath awful. "I'd like to change my will," he said, "make the boy beneficiary."

"All right," Goodloe said.

"I'm obliged," whispered Kirxy. He closed his eyes.

Near the end he was delirious. He said he saw a tiny black creature at the foot of his bed. Said it had him by the toe. In surprising fits of strength, he would throw his water pitcher at it, or his box of tissues, or the *Reader's Digest*. Restraints were called for. His coma was a relief to everyone, and he died quietly in the night.

In Kirxy's chair in the store, Dan didn't seem to hear Goodloe's questions. The sheriff had done some looking in the Grove Hill

Public Library—"research" was the modern word—and discovered that one species of cobra spat venom at its victim's eyes, but there weren't such snakes in southern Alabama. Anyway, the hospital lab had confirmed that it was the poison of a cottonmouth that had blinded Dan. The question, of course, was who had put the venom in his eyes. Goodloe shuddered to think of it, how they'd found Dan staggering about, howling in pain, bleeding from his tear ducts, the skin around his eye sockets dissolving, exposing the white ridges of his skull.

In the investigation, several local blacks including Euphrates Morrisette stated to Goodloe that the youngest Gates boy and his two dead brothers had molested Euphrates's stepdaughter in her own house. There was a rumor that several black men dressed in white sheets with pillowcases for hoods had caught and punished Dan as he lurked along the river, peeping in folks' windows and doing unwholesome things to himself. Others suggested that the conjure woman had cast a spell on the Gateses, that she'd summoned a swamp demon to chase them to hell. And still others attributed the happenings to Frank David. There were a few occurrences of violence between the local whites and the blacks—some fires, a broken jaw—but soon it died down and Goodloe filed the deaths of Kent and Neil Gates as accidental.

But he listed Dan's blinding as unsolved. The snake venom had bleached the boy's pupils white, and the skin around his eye sockets had required grafts. The surgeons had had to use skin from his buttocks, and because his buttocks were hairy, the skin around his eyes began to grow hair, too.

In the years to come, the loggers who clear-cut the land along the river would occasionally stop in the store, less from a need to buy something than from a curiosity to see the hermit with the milky, hairy eyes. The store smelled horrible, like the inside of a bear's mouth, and dust lay thick and soft on the shelves. Because they had come in, the loggers felt obligated to buy something, but every item was moldy or stale beyond belief, except for the things in cans, which were unlabeled so they never knew what they'd get. Nothing was marked as to price, either, and the blind man wouldn't talk. He just sat by the stove. So the loggers paid more (some less) than what they thought a can was worth, leaving the money on the counter by the telephone, which hadn't been connected in years. When plumper, grayer Goodloe came by on the occasional evening, smelling of booze, he'd take the bills and coins and put some in Kirxy's cash drawer and the rest in his pocket. He was no longer sheriff, having lost several elections back to one of his deputies, Roy or Dave. He still wore the same khaki uniform, but now he drove a Lance truck, his route including the hospitals in the county, and, every other month, the prison.

"Dern, boy," he once cracked to Dan. "This store's doing a better business now than it ever has. You sure you don't want you a cookie rack?"

When Goodloe left, Dan listened to the rattle of the truck as it faded. "Sugarbaby," he whispered.

And many a night for years after, until his own death in his sleep, Dan would rise from the chair and move across the floor, taking Kirxy's cane from where it stood by the coatrack. He would go outside, down the stairs like a man who could see, his beard nearly to his belly, and he would walk soundlessly the length of the building, knowing the woods even better now as he crept down the rain-rutted gully side toward the river whose smell never left the caves of his nostrils and the roof of his mouth.

At the riverbank, he would stop and sit with his back against a small pine, and lifting his white eyes to the sky, he would listen to the clicks and hum and thrattle of the woods, seeking out each noise at its source and imagining it: an acorn nodding, detaching, its thin ricochet and the way it settled into the leaves. A bullfrog's bubbling throat and the things it said. The trickle of the river over rocks and around the bases of cattails and cypress knees and through the wet hanging roots of trees. And then another sound, familiar: the soft, precise footsteps of Frank David. Downwind. Not coming closer, not going away. Circling. The striking of a match and the sizzle of ember and fall of ash. The ascent of smoke. A strange and terrifying comfort for the rest of Dan Gates's life.

acknowledgments

Alabama has given me a great varied group of friends, all of whom helped with these stories. My deepest gratitude to Marshall Barth, Laura Cayouette, Charles McNair, Brian Oberkirch and Jack Pendarvis. And to Gary Wolfe, who tells me things like, "Nobody uses lead pipes anymore. You know that."

I was fortunate to live for four splendid years in Fayetteville, Arkansas, where I met Michael Carragher, Jim Colbert, Michael Downs, David Gavin, Otis Haschemeyer, John Reimringer and Sidney "Compson" Thompson. Thanks, guys. Fayetteville also gave me my best reader and best friend: Thanks, B.A., for things only you know. My appreciation, too, to the Arkansas Arts Council for its generous financial support.

I also want to thank Rick Bass, whose stories made me believe in the power of stories; Roy Parvin (burn them dogs); and Paul Ruffin, George Garrett and the staff of *The Texas Review* for taking the chance.

And my teachers. To Skip Hays, Jim Whitehead and Bill Harrison, giants from Arkansas, Mississippi and Texas, respectively; to Joanne Meschery; and (speaking of Texas) to Jim White, one of the most generous men I've ever known: Thank you, thank you, bless you all. . . .

And I owe a special debt of gratitude to Nat Sobel, my agent: Thanks, Nat, for the best wedding present ever. And, for the faith, thanks to Paul Bresnick, my editor; Michael Murphy, my publisher; and the rest of the good folks at William Morrow and Company.

And finally, for gracefully sharing my history, deepest thanks to Barry Bradford, Kenneth Lovell and Jeff Franklin, my brother.